BOLLYWOOD
ACADEMY
1

Starlet Rivals

PUNEET BHANDAL

First published in the United Kingdom in 2022 by Lantana Publishing Ltd., Oxford.
www.lantanapublishing.com | info@lantanapublishing.com

American edition published in 2022 by Lantana Publishing Ltd., UK.

Text © Puneet Bhandal, 2022
Artwork & Design © Lantana Publishing, 2022

Cover and internal illustrations by Jen Khatun

Distributed in the United States and Canada by Lerner Publishing Group, Inc.
241 First Avenue North, Minneapolis, MN 55401 U.S.A.
For reading levels and more, look for this title at www.lernerbooks.com
Cataloging-in-Publication Data Available.

ISBN: 978-1-913747-90-9

Printed and bound in the Czech Republic.

For my dad,
for introducing me to the magical world of Bollywood.

For my mum,
for your unwavering support.

STARLET RIVALS

By Puneet Bhandal

TAKE ONE

I was transfixed. Fully focused on the TV screen. There was pin-drop silence, which was amazing for a room crammed so full of people that there was barely space to move.

"And the winner is..."

"*Eeeeeeeekkkkk...*" I squeezed the arm of my bestie, Priyanka. A little too hard, apparently.

"Ouch!"

"Sorry, Pri!" I said. "I'm just so nervous. It's taking forever!"

"*Shhh!*" said Auntie Brinda from the other end of the sofa.

I was about to answer back but Raman Sood, the TV show host, spoke before I could. "...*Chintu!* Congratulations, Chintu – you're through to the finals!"

The room erupted. There was screaming, shouting, jumping, cheering.

"He's done it!" I yelled, leaping off the sofa. "Oh wow! He's actually done it!"

Chintu had won. The "slum kid" who defied the odds to win five heats of Dance Starz – the biggest TV talent show in India – had bagged a place in the final.

Everyone was buzzing and talking over each other.

"I told you he would do it!" proclaimed Daadi, my grandma. She looked so proud, you'd be forgiven for thinking that Chintu was her own grandson.

"Ma, you always say that – no matter who wins!" my dad shot back.

I grabbed a corner of Priyanka's T-shirt, tugging her towards the door. "Let's go to my room," I whispered, edging past Auntie Poonam who had started waving her arms around in an impression of Chintu's winning dance.

"What are we gonna do when the show's over?" Priyanka asked as she planted herself on my bed. She lifted my new eyeshadow palette off my dresser and got to work on my eyelids. She was great at makeup, while I was terrible, and she always insisted on giving me a makeover when she came to visit. "I love Dance Starz so much. Chintu was just...amazing! I mean, how is he so flexible? Those back flips!"

Priyanka wasn't the only one who had been swept up in the talent show's craze. Even though this was the first season, it seemed that there wasn't a single family in India that wasn't glued to their screens on Friday nights.

I had seen every episode. Sometimes, when I was in

my room alone, I would pretend I was on the show. I'd do the whole routine, imagining someone was introducing me, and then I'd dance and fantasize that the crowd was going wild for my performance.

Priyanka continued to sweep the shimmery green eyeshadow across my lids, taking a step back to check her work.

"You know, you should have entered, Bela," she said. "You could have been on your way to fame and riches."

I opened my eyes wide.

"Keep them shut!" she scolded.

"Are you crazy?" I asked. "Me? Enter Dance Starz? I mean, yes, I'm classically trained, but these TV shows want that modern, stunt kind of dancing. I can't even do a single back flip!"

Priyanka laughed. "It's a dance show, not a circus!" She snapped the little box of shimmer shut. "You're a great dancer, Bela. I don't know anyone as good as you."

I smiled. She always championed me, even though I was nowhere near as good as she thought I was. Priyanka was the definition of BFF.

I walked over to the dressing table mirror to admire my new look.

"Mmmm, smells *soooo* good," stated Priyanka, closing her eyes and taking a deep whiff of the smell of freshly cooked samosas wafting over from the kitchen.

"Bela! Priyanka!" came Mom's voice as if on cue. "Food is ready. *Here, now!*" Mom was always calling somebody in the household to come and eat. It was funny how she used the same come-and-eat tone each time.

We walked into the kitchen which was a carnival of aromas and animated chatter. Each auntie talked louder than the next, as though the louder they spoke, the greater the importance of their opinion. The funny thing was that they weren't even my real aunties. I always wondered whether India was the only place where kids addressed every adult as "auntie" or "uncle" out of respect.

"Come girls, sit," Mom said, frowning a little when she noticed my eyeshadow. She always told me I was too young for makeup but she was the one who had bought it for me as a treat for performing to her students the week before. I'd danced to *Tap To My Heartbeat* – the hit song of the year. It was ridiculously catchy with its Hindi verses and English chorus against a disco beat.

Apart from being an outstanding dance teacher, Mom was the best cook in our neighborhood. People were always telling her to start a food business, but with her full-time job as a teaching assistant while also running weekend dance classes, she just didn't have the time.

Priyanka tucked in while I nabbed two of the smallest samosas. I was known as a picky eater – just like my sister, Zara, who came and parked herself in my lap.

"Zara, do you have to?" I chided. It was way too hot to have a sticky six-year-old in your lap.

Mom shot me a glance – the glance that said, "She's your younger sister. You must look after her."

"*When I was your age, I looked after all 4000 of my younger siblings...*" I whispered to Priyanka, mimicking Mom's voice.

Priyanka and I giggled, while Zara slid off my lap and ran away. We grabbed our plates, walked through our narrow, tiled hallway, and went and sat on the front doorstep.

There was no respite from the heat outside but at least it felt less claustrophobic. The near-hysterical chitter chatter of the aunties dimmed just a little. I couldn't blame Dad for going into his room and closing the door behind him.

"Hey, Bela," said Rimpi, Auntie Brinda's eight-year-old daughter and our next-door neighbor. She was on her bike, wearing a frilly pink party dress and somehow expertly gripping the pedals with her rubber flip-flops.

"Did you see the end of the show?" she asked, looking

at my plate.

I shook my head. "No, I'm recording it to watch later," I replied, dipping a corner of my samosa in the homemade chutney. I offered her the other one, which she politely declined.

"Shashi Kumar said he wants one more contestant for the final. So they're doing a wild show."

"Wait, what? You mean a wild card show?" I asked, glancing at Priyanka.

"Yes, that's it!" squealed Rimpi. "It's video entry. Shashi Kumar said that because so many people couldn't travel for the live auditions, they're going to do one more round and find one more finalist. All you have to do is send a video to the Dance Starz website. The best one gets into the final."

Priyanka and I looked at each other again. She was beaming from ear to ear. I knew exactly what she was thinking.

"Shashi Kumar also said that the finalist will be allowed to bring friends and family members to the actual live event!" our little informer added excitedly. "He said he wants to fill the arena with people who can't pay for a ticket."

Ever since Shashi Kumar – former Bollywood hero-turned-movie producer – had launched Dance Starz, he seemed to be on every radio and TV show going, and he never wasted a single opportunity to mention the prize. The overall winner of Dance Starz would score a place at the most prestigious stage school in the Eastern world: the Bollywood Academy.

The school, owned by Shashi Kumar and other VIPs, was on Kohinoor Island, a thirty-minute crossing from Mumbai. It was still in its first year but was already attended by lots of rich and famous kids, including Shashi's daughter – child star and model, Monica. The fees were eye-watering, but the message was that you were pretty much guaranteed a job in the industry once you graduated.

To get into that kind of school would be a *really* big deal.

Priyanka put her plate down. She stood up and pointed at me. "You know exactly what you have to do, Bela. For me, for Rimpi, for our school, for our neighborhood. For us!"

If she didn't become a makeup artist, Priyanka would make a great politician.

"Please, Bela! Please!" begged Rimpi, clasping her hands together. "You're the best dancer in the whole street. The whole neighborhood! The whole town! You're the best dancer in the world!"

I smiled at Rimpi. Even though she was clearly exaggerating, it was still flattering.

A couple of local boys who were playing soccer in the alleyway outside must have heard the elevated shrieking and, before long, I was cornered.

"Do it, man! Just send a video!" encouraged Mujeeb, doing kick-ups as he spoke. He had been in my brother Reuben's class at primary school and they were still close.

"What's all the commotion for?" said Mom, suddenly appearing behind me. "Samosa, Mujeeb?" she asked, holding her plate up towards him and his pal.

"No thanks, Auntie," he said politely, before explaining what was going on.

Mom's eyes widened as he spoke. A dance fanatic herself, she had desperately wanted me to audition for the show from the day it was launched, almost four months earlier. She had told me over and over again not to let the opportunity slip by – that it was "now or never." Contestants had to be under thirteen; I had just turned twelve. I guess she was right on that front.

But I really didn't think it was ever going to become such a big deal and, despite everyone always telling me how awesome I was, I was *no way* good enough to be on national TV.

Now though, I couldn't help but mull it over. Ever

since I was four years old, I'd told anybody who would listen that I wanted to be an Indian film star when I grew up. A place at the Bollywood Academy might just be my ticket in.

"But what if I do badly?" I said, once everyone around me had stopped talking. "I obviously won't win. It'll be embarrassing! I mean, I can't compete with these kids, Mom, can I?"

Mom's face lit up. She sensed I was caving in. "You might surprise yourself," she smiled. "It could be a once-in-a-lifetime opportunity. I wish I'd had these chances when I was young..."

I groaned. The number of times I'd heard that.

"Even if you don't win," reasoned Priyanka, "you might as well enter. It's so easy to make a two-minute video."

"Do it for your daadi!" Mom added. "She won't be here forever." Emotional blackmail was Mom's special talent.

She saw the expression on my face.

"Okay, fine," she said. "I'll get you a cell phone if you do it."

"Really?" I stood up.

"Yes, really," she agreed.

"An iPhone?"

Mom glared at me.

"Fine! I'll do it," I announced, not quite believing what I was saying. "But I won't win. *No way* will I get into the finals against all those super talented kids."

They didn't care much about that part. Nobody was looking that far ahead. All they heard was that I was willing to enter the competition and that they were in with a chance of being in the live studio audience.

Mom ran back inside to share the news with Daadi and the neighborhood gossip girls and it wasn't long before I heard whooping and cheering from the kitchen.

Next, I heard the sound of Zara's little feet as she ran toward me. "*Belaaaaaaaaaa!* You're gonna be on Dance Starz!" she screamed as she put her arms around my waist.

Priyanka grabbed both of us and gave us the tightest hug ever. "You won't regret it, Bela, I promise!"

I wasn't so sure about that but I sincerely hoped she was right.

TAKE TWO

The next day, I was woken by the sounds of the street outside. Our neighborhood, Sector R2 in the suburb of Chandivali, North Central Mumbai, was always bustling. Car horns were honking and music was blaring from the taxi drivers and rickshawalas scuttling past.

Chandivali was famous as a mini Silicon Valley. Lots of tech companies had sprung up there recently and it was modernizing fast. Little rows of houses with small front and rear gardens were springing up on every spare patch of unused land. Daadi hated the pace at which Chandivali was changing. She was particularly sad that the small chai sellers had been forced to leave to make way for national coffee chains.

My eyes kept closing and I couldn't stop hitting the snooze button on my alarm clock until Mom burst in and pulled my comforter off. "Up you get!" she said. "You know we have to upload the video by this evening. Which means filming NOW!"

I bolted out of bed. Mom meant business. While I was hurriedly getting changed, I wondered if I was doing the right thing. Then, I remembered. Firstly, Mom would finally get me a phone if I went ahead and, secondly, there was a teeny weeny chance that even if I didn't get on the show, perhaps a big movie producer would spot me and offer me a movie role?

"Mom, can I borrow your cell to message my friends?" I puffed as I scraped my hair into a high ponytail.

She handed it to me with the usual: "Straight back to me when you're done."

I clicked the messaging icon and sent pics to my best friends – Priyanka, Ayesha and Reshma – who had all sent me texts to make sure I wouldn't change my mind.

"No, Ayesha, I won't chicken out! And yes, Reshma, I will wear that sparkly red jumpsuit!" I wrote back. Reshma was the fashion guru in our gang.

Uncle Manoj – Rimpi's dad and Auntie Brinda's husband – had volunteered to film my segment. He was Sector R2's party photographer and had the snazziest video camera of anyone I knew.

I grabbed Zara's hand. The ten-minute walk to the dance studio always seemed longer when you had a little kid in tow.

"Come on, Za," I said. She shuffled and ran to keep up.

"Walk faster, please," Mom urged, her tan brown sandals kicking up dust as she steamed ahead. "I have so much to do when I get back home."

I rolled my eyes. Like I'd had to beg and plead with Mom to do this!

As soon as we arrived, I put on my spangly, stretch jumpsuit. Mom then expertly created a bun out of my waist-length hair and secured it with bobby pins.

Because we didn't have time to prepare a brand-new routine, I decided I would dance to *Tap To My Heartbeat*. The funky disco moves were still fresh in my mind and the song was so popular I hoped it would help sway the voters – especially the younger ones.

Priyanka, Ayesha and Reshma had taken the front row, clapping and waiting for me to start. Uncle Manoj was at the ready, camera perched on a stand. Rimpi and Auntie Brinda were sitting a few seats behind my friends.

Zara was standing up on one side of the hall. No doubt she would try to mimic my moves from the floor. Zara was so cute and tiny but already an accomplished dancer. She, like me, had joined Mom's dance classes as soon as she turned two. "There is no time to waste. We have something new to learn each day!" Mom would tell us. It was like a mantra.

The music started and I struck my pose, one leg raised in front of the other. My left hand was fanned out in front of my face and my right arm at full stretch to the side, fingers upturned. Although I was standing on one leg, I was perfectly balanced; dance had given me great core strength.

I didn't feel any nerves – this stage was like my own personal playground. I'd started dancing there almost as soon as I had learned to walk. The studio felt like a second home to me.

As always, when I danced, my body felt like it was being moved by some inner power. I didn't need to think much about what I was doing, I just felt it. Mom had given me classical training but we loved to merge the traditional movements of Bharatanatyam – the oldest dance form in India – with modern Bollywood or Western steps. This was my happy place. I could seamlessly shift between them at the flick of a switch.

I savored the experience with my whole being, embracing the stage, feeling the music and miming to the lyrics of the peppy Bollywood hit. I could see my mom urging me on, nodding her head in approval as I expertly performed the steps she had taught me.

Unashamedly, I was also enjoying the full attention of those watching. I pretended I was the closing act at a Bollywood awards show, imagining hundreds of people watching me, whistling and clapping.

Trouble was, it seemed to be over in a flash. I wanted

to carry on. I could literally perform all day, all night.

I looked straight at Mom when I was done. Only her expression could tell me how good I had been. She quickly got up, climbed the few steps leading to the stage, and gave me a gigantic hug.

"Wonderful, Bela! You make me so proud," she whispered into my ear as my private audience rose to their feet and applauded.

I loved to see my mom's face light up each time I finished a performance. I knew she would have grabbed the chance to compete in Dance Starz with both hands at my age. Perhaps living it through me was the next best thing.

She was happy. I was happy. Maybe this wasn't such a bad idea, after all.

*

"I don't want the whole neighborhood coming round, Mom!" I huffed.

"It'll be fun, beti. Auntie Brinda said she will make pakoras for us," said Mom.

"I don't care about pakoras," I shot back.

"I love pakoras!" interjected Zara, who was dressed in a shiny Wonder Woman costume complete with headband and armbands. "*Pleeeeease*, Bela, let Auntie Brinda come! I want to play with Rimpi."

I got up off the sofa and went into my room.

Things were getting out of control. I'd agreed to enter the Dance Starz wild card show mainly because I wanted a phone. And that part was done – Mom had promised I would get one over the summer vacation.

Yes, I also wanted to have an outside chance of getting spotted by a Bollywood bigwig, but I wasn't counting on it. The whole neighborhood was acting as though I had made it onto the show. I felt weighed down by their expectations.

The wild card show was due to be streamed live the following Sunday. Dad had uploaded my video the day before after some nifty editing by Uncle Manoj. We had then been informed by email that over the course of the week, members of the public would vote for their favorite entry, and the Top 10 would feature live on the show.

Although I didn't expect to win, I didn't want to lose in a humiliating fashion either. Daadi and I had sneaked a peek at some of the entries but I couldn't really tell where my performance ranked in comparison. Dance Starz was cleverly keeping the number of votes each video was getting secret.

I picked up my pastel-colored unicorn teddy and

began combing its fluffy hair. Mom always laughed when she saw me doing this, but it relaxed me.

"Bela," said Dad, peering around the door before coming over and sitting on the bed next to me. There was a telling-off coming – I could feel it. Dad only ever came into my room when he wanted to lecture me.

"We won't let anybody come over on Sunday evening if you don't want them to," he said softly.

I looked up. No lecture?

"You can invite your friends around, but don't worry if you don't feel like it. It's a little unfair to make such a big deal of this. Maybe we shouldn't have pressured you to enter."

"I want to invite my friends over," I told him. "But can we watch the show on your laptop in my bedroom?"

Dad must have been feeling really generous because he agreed, despite never letting any of us touch his precious laptop. We all had to use the ancient tablet. To call it temperamental would be an understatement.

"What about Mom, though? She has high hopes of eating Auntie Brinda's pakoras..."

"Don't worry about Auntie Brinda's pakoras," said Dad, laughing. "Maybe we can send Mom over to her house instead?"

We high-fived. I loved that idea. I didn't admit it to

Dad, but I felt more nervous with the idea of Mom being around. She was the one who had painstakingly taught me how to dance. Failing in front of her would be the most painful way to fail.

Mom got the hint. She gave me a big hug at 6pm on Sunday evening. "Don't worry about the result, Bela," she said as she stepped outside. "We'll be proud of you whatever happens." Even so, I could sense her excitement bubbling underneath the calm exterior. She had a bag full of snacks to take next door to Auntie Brinda's. All of the gossip girls would be there. Mom said the show was a perfect excuse for a girly get-together.

"I want to stay *heeere*," moaned Zara as Mom dragged her away by the hand. "Why can't I stay with Bela and her friends?"

"Don't worry, Zizi," I said. I called her that when I was being extra affectionate. "You'll be back before you know it."

Zara kept her gaze down. She always did that when she was sulking.

"And we can make a dance reel and post on Mom's Instagram when you get back."

"Yay!" She jumped up and down.

"Only on my private account," Mom snapped at me. I rolled my eyes and Zara laughed, before waving at me as they walked off.

It was now time for my own girly get-together. Priyanka, as usual, was the first to arrive, followed by Reshma and Ayesha who arrived together. We had all been friends since the age of three. We'd been in the same class since preschool. And living within five minutes' walk of each other meant we were in and out of each other's houses all the time. The hashtag #friendslikefamily was us.

"Guys, don't get too excited," I said as the girls took off their shoes in preparation for snuggling up on the bed. "I don't even think my video will make the Top 10, in which case they won't even air it on tonight's show."

"Of course you're gonna make the show!" said Ayesha confidently. She was so smart – she rarely got anything wrong at school. I hoped she was right about this too. "Have you seen some of the videos? Not being mean but, seriously! Some are just so bad."

"She's right," added Reshma, wagging her finger. "I've been keeping an eye on the entries." She held up the phone her dad had given her – it was her most prized possession. "Looking at the competition, your performance is miles better! You could be famous by tomorrow morning!"

The girls giggled but my stomach was doing a dance

routine of its own. I took a deep breath just as Reuben walked past with a big plate of pizza and a fizzing glass of cola. He went into his room and closed the door.

"Is he even watching it?" asked Priyanka.

"Doubt it," I replied. "He's always too busy gaming." Reuben never hung around when my friends were over. Ever since he'd turned fourteen, it was like he was suddenly too cool to be around us. I wouldn't ever admit it to him, but sometimes I missed my big brother.

"Evening, girls," said Dad cheerily. He was carrying his laptop. "I'm going to set this up for you and then I'll be in my room if you need me."

"Thanks, Dad," I smiled. I had butterflies in my stomach – a mix of nerves and anticipation.

Daadi came in with some plates of crisps and Indian sweets. "Yum! I love jalebis," said Ayesha, helping herself. "Thank you, Boss!" That was the name my friends had given my daadi. She really was the boss, even if she didn't look like one. She was half our size and always wore off-white or cream-colored cotton sarees wrapped tightly around her small frame. She wore them a little high so her ankles were on display.

"Can I sit with you?" asked Daadi.

I looked at my friends. Then I felt bad that I'd hesitated. Daadi was so sweet, she'd never make me feel bad even if I came last.

I nodded.

"Boss!" said Priyanka affectionately, patting the bed next to her. "Come and sit next to me."

We all lined up on the bed while Dad set up the computer. My friends tucked into the snacks, but I was way too nervous to eat. I got up and paced around the room, hands in the pockets of my sweatpants.

"I think I'm still confused about the rules," Dad said.

"Basically, Uncle," began Ayesha while Dad finished typing in the website address, "the videos have been up for seven days and the public has been voting. The ten videos with the most votes go through to the live wild card show."

"Oh," he said. "I thought it was all going to happen live?"

"No," chipped in Priyanka. "There are way too many entries! We'd be here all night! At 7pm, the top ten videos will be played, and each judge will give a score out of 10. The contestant with the highest score goes through to the final."

I looked at the clock and my stomach did a somersault when I realized that there were just five minutes to go till 7pm. Would I make the shortlist? What if my video wasn't even there?

We sat back and waited. Then the familiar theme tune filled the room and the host, Raman Sood, appeared in a dazzling sequined suit – his trademark.

"Enjoy!" said Dad, giving me a "Good luck, don't worry" squeeze before disappearing down the corridor.

I felt sick.

"Thank you for joining us for this special live show," enthused Raman. "And a massive thank you to all those who entered. We've had hundreds of entries. Unfortunately, we can't show you all of them. But let's find out which ones made it into the Top 10!"

We watched as the first two-minute video was aired. The contestant was really good. She chose Kathak – a dance form originating in the north of India – and used lots of hand movements and facial expressions. The high-profile judging panel was made up of eight big names from TV, the movies and the press, including the Principal of the Bollywood Academy. They gave their score: 56, which I felt was a little low.

I was beginning to hope my video wouldn't be aired, when I spotted someone on the screen.

"Who's that girl?" I asked, pointing to her as the next video was about to play. "On the panel, sitting next to Shashi Kumar?" She looked familiar but I couldn't place her.

"That's Monica," said Daadi. "Shashi Kumar's daughter. Bhushan Kumar's granddaughter. She was in that TV series. I forget the name..."

"*House Party*, Boss!" said Ayesha.

"Yes! That's the one," Daadi responded with a clap of her hands.

"That's Monica?" I was astonished. I'd seen her in *House Party* too but that was maybe five years ago, when she was six or seven years old. I used to pretend she was my best friend. I'd sit with my toys and imagine we were playing together. She looked much older now and very different.

"She's the same age as us," said Ayesha. "One of my Dad's friends' brother's sons goes to the Bollywood Academy and he's in her class."

I was trying to process all of this when I was jolted out of my thoughts by the first few beats of the next video. I looked up and caught sight of myself on screen. A small shriek escaped my lips.

"Look! Look!" Reshma was screaming. "You *did* make the Top 10!"

Priyanka got up off the bed and crouched in front of the laptop, clapping enthusiastically. Daadi stood up to dance, copying my moves, while Dad and Reuben ran into the room to join us.

"What happened? What happened?" cried Reuben. I couldn't remember seeing him that excited since he'd gotten his first gaming console.

I pointed at the screen. "Nothing yet. But it's being aired. I made the shortlist!" I covered my face with my hands and peeked through my fingers.

Dad came and stood behind me. Nobody was sitting any more. The camera flashed over to the judging table as they all started scribbling.

My heart was in my mouth. I felt like I was going to faint. I couldn't watch.

I ran off into Reuben's room and closed the door behind me. I could hear my friends calling my name.

"Bela!"

"It's fine!"

"Come!"

But I refused. I sat on the bed, arms crossed tightly. Suddenly, there was raucous yelling.

"That's my girl!" cheered Dad.

"She's nailed it!" cried Daadi.

"Yes, Boss!" shouted Ayesha.

I ran back inside, scouring their faces, looking at the screen.

"You're literally getting all 10s!"

Daadi hugged me tight, her glasses digging into me.

"You have to win now," she said. "No one else has got straight 10s."

I watched as Monica held up her score card: "8."

We all looked at each other.

"Ok, beti, you got all 10s except for that 8."

"What's her problem?" asked Reshma, taking it very personally.

I was still reeling from all the 10s. I mean, how was that even possible? From such a distinguished panel?

We stopped to watch the next few videos playing out. One of the contestants was seriously good. We gasped as she pirouetted in the air and finished her performance with the splits.

Despite her acrobatics, I sensed I would be hard to beat when we got to video eight and nobody had even come close to my score.

I could sense the excitement building around me.

Dad was on the phone to Mom from his bedroom and Reuben was texting his friends as he sat on the floor in front of the computer.

"This is crazy," said Reuben. "This show is trending on Twitter... Oh wow – *you're* trending on Twitter!"

It wasn't long before Mom and Zara came bursting in through the front door.

"What's happening? What's happening?" Mom

screeched as she rushed into my bedroom. She went straight to the laptop, eyes wide open.

"Bela – you've won!" said Dad.

"Has she?" asked Mom.

"Of course she has," said Reuben. "Unless somebody got 80. Bela's score is 78."

I was confused. What was going on?

"As some of you may have worked out, the winner of the Dance Starz wild card show for a place in the final is...BELA KHANNA!"

Chaos ensued.

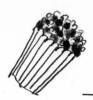

TAKE THREE

The phone started ringing and it just didn't stop. Our house was taken over by all of Sector R2. People came in and out, taking turns to congratulate me. My friends were celebrating wildly, singing and dancing with Daadi and taking lots of photos. Reuben was jumping up and down and yelling in his newly-acquired deep voice.

I was still in shock. I literally couldn't believe I had won the wild card show! Could this really be happening?

Zara jumped on me and hugged me tighter than I knew a six-year-old could squeeze. Rimpi was beaming from ear to ear and just staring at me, like she was awestruck. It was weird.

I gave Uncle Manoj an extra-big hug. He'd made the video, after all. Maybe that was why I'd won?

"All the other entries – the quality was so bad," said Auntie Brinda, looking admiringly at her husband. "Bela's video was so good. So professionally shot."

Mom was now on her phone, posting on her Dance_ With_Shanta Instagram account and tagging the show. She was already getting more followers off the back of the result.

"And why not, Shanta?" Dad told her. "You deserve credit. You're the one who taught this dance champion." He ruffled my hair.

I smiled. I wasn't quite a dance champion and I wasn't sure I ever would be. But coming first at something so big with so many famous people on the panel felt good. And to see all my loved ones reveling in my victory was the icing on the cake.

I was on a high for the next few hours. I couldn't switch off even when I went to bed that night. I don't know when I finally fell asleep but it certainly wasn't for as long as I needed. Especially with the early morning wake-up call I had.

"Yes, yes, you must all come for a vacation soon," Mom was yelling down the phone. She was talking to my Canadian cousins at some ungodly hour. It seemed like everyone, including all of Dad's family who still lived in villages far away, had called to congratulate me. Mom had even spoken to relatives I didn't know I had.

I wanted to sleep, but my mind kept trying to process everything that had happened. Was I really going to be in the final of Dance Starz? Or was this all some bizarre dream that I was going to wake up from soon?

I must have dozed off.

"Hurry up, hurry up!" Mom was saying while running

around the house. "I still have to make the lunches. Bela, please grab the water bottles and help your sister brush her teeth."

I groaned and buried my head under my comforter. Mom was over in a flash to rip it off. She gave me The Stare and I knew it was game over.

Zara and I literally sprinted the half mile to school to get there on time. I had no idea how Mom ran so fast in her sandals while holding our backpacks, water bottles, lunch boxes and her purse too. She ushered us in and vanished off to her day job.

I was out of breath by the time I reached my classroom. I turned the door handle very slowly, knowing I was late and hoping I would be able to slip in quietly without anyone noticing.

"Hooray! It's the superstar!"

"Dance Star Bela!"

I was startled. The whole class was standing up, applauding and shouting my name.

I blushed. Mrs. Ahuja, my teacher, came over and gave me a big hug. "Congratulations, Bela," she beamed. "You've made us all so proud. Can you believe it? Our little school – famous!"

I looked perplexed until she explained that several TV stations had already visited the school that morning to interview staff and students about my victory.

"Bela, you're going to be rich and famous now," said Chandu, one of the smartest boys in class. "Will you still remember us when you're at the Bollywood Academy?"

"I don't think I can win the final," I said, cheeks burning.

"Oh no?" said another of my classmates, waving a newspaper at me.

My eyes widened when I saw the front page. In the bottom right-hand corner of the Mumbai Central Chronicle – our biggest local paper – was a photo of me from the video performance. The headline read:

A RAGS TO RICHES TALE OR A FLASH IN THE PAN?

Firstly, what did "a flash in the pan" even mean? Secondly, the word "rags" was outright rude! I didn't dress in rags!

I looked at my teacher.

"Okay, everyone, that's enough. Time for the register," she said, clapping loudly so that everyone would take their seats. "But a final round of applause for Bela who has done herself, her family, and the whole school proud."

I sat down in my chair and felt more on edge than I'd ever felt in my life. I couldn't work out why. Everything was happening so fast.

Suddenly, there was so much expectation. Everyone really thought I could win this.

But would I be able to deliver?

*

"You need to keep them away from newspapers and social media," I could hear Dad telling Mom. I crept over to their bedroom door so I could listen in.

"Yes, I know that, Uday, but kids will hear everything from their friends anyway," Mom replied. "And I mean, apart from that nasty news story where we were made out to be a beggar family," she added, obviously stinging from the same article that had shocked me, "the attention hasn't been so bad."

"Hmm," said Dad, with an undertone of annoyance. "I'm wondering whether she should have entered the show in the first place," he said. "The other day, when Bela and I went to get fruit from the market, I swear someone was taking photos of us."

"So what?" snapped Mom. "That's what happens when you get famous! You have to deal with it."

"Famous?" he scoffed. "We're not famous! Bela hasn't even won the competition. It's only been a week since she got put through. Even if she does win, even if she gets the scholarship, there's no guarantee of fame."

"Be negative then," Mom said, "but I've always known Bela has what it takes. Her star shines so bright, it was only a matter of time before she got spotted."

I scuttled back to the living room and flung myself on the sofa when I heard her footsteps.

I picked up the tablet and took a photo of myself with the craziest filter I could find and sent it to Ayesha. I got one back almost instantly – Ayesha looked hilarious as a piece of toast!

"What are you laughing at?" asked Zara, running over and sitting so close she was literally stuck to me.

"Nothing, Zara," I said, lifting the tablet up so she couldn't see. This was between me and my friends.

"Will you play with me?" she asked in her cutest, tiniest little voice while tugging at her pig tails.

I was about to bark at her to go away when Mom floated past. She gave me The Stare. She always seemed to know exactly what I was going to say and do next.

"Yes! I'll play with you," I said eventually, trying to disguise my annoyance. "But only for ten minutes, okay? I have dance practice again, don't you know? What else do I do except school, sleep, dance and eat these days, huh? Mom thinks I'm a machine."

In the final, I would be dancing to *Ek Baar Dance With Me* – a really famous Bollywood song that was around five years old. I was doing an entirely original dance routine. "Copied moves won't cut it," Mom had insisted. She said I needed to be authentic, and I agreed. I mean, there was no way I was going to compete in acrobatics or street dance with the likes of Chintu! I had to be true to *me*.

Mom had choreographed a routine from scratch, combining traditional elements of Bharatanatyam with Bollywood's modern, Western style. It was easier said than done – you could get it horribly wrong. But Mom was an expert at her craft. If there was a competition for fusion dance styles, she would win hands down.

"I really need to practice, Zara," I said.

Zara looked at me with her sad puppy dog eyes.

"Don't give me that look!" I said, pointing right at her. "I'm stressed as it is. Everyone expects me to win and I know I won't. I was put under so much pressure to be in the show and now everyone's talking about how we're poor and how we wear rags and it's so embarrassing." I didn't intend to blurt that out. It must have been playing on my mind.

Mom, who was busily doing the dusting, heard me and walked over.

"Don't pay attention to any of that, Bela," she said, waving a lime green fluffy duster in my face. "Social media and newspapers operate at gutter level these days."

"But you don't know what it's like for me! It's fine for you. I'm the one they all talk about at school," I complained. "I don't want anyone to know where we live or what we wear."

I folded my arms tightly both because I was annoyed and to stop Zara tugging at me to get up.

"*I* want to be in the competition. It's not fair that I can't do it," she moaned, bottom lip jutting out in full sulk mode.

"Urgh! I can't even..." I stormed off into my room and slammed the door behind me.

Why was I so angry? It wasn't really Mom's fault or Zara's fault. I'd agreed to enter the competition after all. I looked around my small and modest room. I'd always considered myself lucky to have my own room. So many of my friends shared with siblings or slept on sofa beds in living rooms. Trouble was, it didn't look so inviting anymore. I imagined what the bedroom of a child star like Monica would be like. It would be huge. Maybe she had one of those walk-in wardrobes like they have on US celebrity shows?

A pile of Bollywood magazines sat neatly in one corner. Daadi bought me one almost every time she went into town. I read them cover to cover and then added them to the precious pile. Posters of top Bollywood stars including Zain Khan, SriLata and Rocky were blu-tacked to my walls.

I picked up my unicorn and started combing its hair. There had been so much excitement and hype around me for the past few days. Now that the dust was starting to settle, I was feeling troubled by other thoughts. I mean, making it through to the final was wild alright. But now that I was there, would I actually be able to compete against all those contestants who had battled through five rounds?

I gulped and felt a cold sensation envelop me. I was nowhere near their level, was I? The newspapers had called me "flash in the pan." Maybe that was true. Maybe I would be here today, gone tomorrow. I mean, people like Chintu had so many fans, legitimately gained over so many months. I felt like a bit of a fraud. One comment on social media had even said that I cheated my way into the competition.

"Mom," I said, walking into the kitchen where she was now cooking. "Do you really think I'm good enough to be in the final?"

Mom added a knob of butter to her daal. She leaned over the pan to smell the delicious lentil soup, then wiped her hands on her apron, switched the cooker off, and turned to me. "If only you could see what I see in you," she sighed. "But you're young, and you can't."

She paused for a moment, and then announced: "Your *Tap To My Heartbeat* performance was technically perfect."

My jaw dropped. "It was?"

For Mom to call my dance perfect was like getting the highest grade in an exam. She was so critical of everybody in her class. Some students had even quit because they couldn't meet her sky-high expectations.

"You never told me that before," I said, clasping my hands together and sitting upright.

"No, because I don't ever want you to get too big for your britches or think you're too good to practice. Maybe you're lucky that you didn't have to go through five rounds. But on that day, on my stage, you made zero mistakes."

"So why did Monica give me an 8?" I asked. I hadn't been able to fathom why Monica had been less impressed by my performance than the other judges.

"Well," Mom began, hesitating as though working out

what to say. "Firstly, that girl had *no* business being on that show."

The force with which Mom said it surprised me. Even Reuben, who was hovering outside the kitchen typing frantically into his phone, looked up.

"What's with the anger, Mom?" he joked.

"I'm serious!" said Mom. "Monica is, what, eleven or twelve years old herself? Why was she a judge? Because she was in a TV sitcom as a kid and has done some child modeling due to her parents' star status."

Mom was using her angry energy to scrub down the kitchen counter.

"Well, she knows nothing – *zero, nada* – about dance. Bela has been training for nine whole years, six hours a week. Nobody with any knowledge about dance or any sense would have given her anything less than a full score."

Reuben looked at me. "Yeah, I guess Bela's not so bad," he said with a wink.

I tried to elbow him but he blocked me. His reflexes were far better than mine.

I was so bolstered by Mom's praise, I felt like a heavy weight had been lifted. When it came to dance, I trusted nobody more.

If Mom felt I was good enough, then I needed to

believe it too.

*

It all started to feel even more real when I received an email inviting me to a dress fitting ahead of the Dance Starz final.

Zara wanted to come with me, as usual. It wasn't until Dad offered to take her to see the latest Disney Pixar movie that she stopped grouching.

Daadi had gone off to Hyderabad for a couple of weeks to spend time with her sister's family, and Reuben was probably in bed. He didn't get up before 2pm on the weekends.

Mom, who literally wore makeup once a year, was expertly applying winged eyeliner and a dark brown lipstick. It suited her mint floral dress perfectly.

"That looks so nice," I said, fleetingly wondering whether my jeans and T-shirt were too casual. "What's the occasion?"

She elbowed me. "I'm so nervous at the possibility of seeing Shashi Kumar and Malaika Rani. They were the biggest stars when I was growing up. I can still remember buying magazines to see their wedding photos twenty years ago!"

Uncle Manoj offered to drive us to Blockbuster Studios in South Mumbai since we didn't have our own car. We were always so grateful to him for offering.

Forty minutes later, thanks to a knack for avoiding busy routes and a knowledge of the back streets, he announced that we'd arrived. From the street, you'd picture the most ordinary building behind the slightly rusty metal gates, but it was nothing like that once you were inside. Blockbuster Studios, owned by Shashi Kumar, of course, was a big sprawling estate.

We drove up to the main building, passing perfect-looking palm trees and some smaller outbuildings which all appeared to be editing suites and sound studios judging by their signs. We pulled into a "Visitor" parking space. I was thrilled. I'd never been inside a movie studio before.

"We have to show them we're not the 'commoners' they tried to make us out to be," whispered Mom as we stepped out of the car. "Make sure you say 'please' and 'thank you.'"

I nodded while keenly surveying the reception area of the building as we walked in. Would the other finalists be here? I wondered what they would make of me. Would they be irritated that I had been fast-tracked to the final? My excitement was giving way to anxiety.

The receptionist pointed toward a smartly-dressed assistant who led us down a corridor to an area marked "Dressing Rooms."

"Please take a seat. The designer Mayuri Jain will be with you in a moment," she stated before neatly click-clacking away.

"Mayuri Jain!" Mom gasped.

I was confused. Was I supposed to know who she was?

"You don't know Mayuri?"

I shook my head.

"She's only *the* famous dress designer who *all* the top movie stars go to for their outfits!"

"Oh..." I replied, still not getting it.

"Hi!" called a man as he rushed past.

It took me a second to register who he was. I felt like someone had pressed pause on my brain and I was unable to speak for a few seconds.

"Oh... Oh... Mom!"

She looked quizzically at me.

"That was Raman Sood! The Dance Starz host!"

"Was it?" Mom replied. "He looks much shorter in real life. Oh, what a shame we missed him! I would have asked him for a selfie."

A few more children walked into the waiting area with adults in tow. I recognized all the contestants from the Dance Starz preliminaries. Mom gently nudged me to stop staring. I had to remind myself to avoid looking star-struck. I was supposed to be competing with them!

"Good afternoon," came a rather fancy-sounding voice.

"Ma'am," Mom said, rising from her seat.

Urgh, cringe-factor off the scale! I hated it when Mom called people "ma'am." It was so British Raj.

"Mayuri Jain," said the designer, introducing herself.

I was immediately struck by her outfit choice – purple suede ankle boots, dark green studded jeans and a purple glittery T-shirt. It all seemed highly questionable but somehow it worked. She was beautiful, in an unconventional way. She had a heart-shaped face, narrow eyes, a very straight, sharp nose and a natural pout.

Mom nervously shook her hand and nodded. "Nice to m...m...meet you."

"Are you the winner of the wild card show?" Mayuri asked, squinting a little to make her narrow eyes even narrower.

I nodded.

"Ah, I love a rags-to-riches fairy tale," she commented, beckoning us to follow her. I looked at Mom and grimaced. Mom shook her head, basically telling me to keep my mouth shut.

"I was born into a film family," she added, completely unnecessarily, "so it's nice to hear about outsiders trying to break in."

Outsiders? Breaking in? I gulped. Was that what people thought I was doing?

We followed Mayuri down another long corridor. She opened the door to a room with the sign "VIP ACCESS ONLY" and I let out a squeal. I couldn't believe the dressing room! It was the most fabulous space I'd ever seen. Gold mirrors hung from velvet-papered walls and the furniture looked like the stuff you see on one of those crazy real estate shows on TV. The red leather sofa in the shape of lips made me laugh.

Mayuri led us to a row of dresses. She looked me up and down, a bit like an annoying auntie who disapproves of what you're wearing. "What song will you be dancing to?"

"*Ek Baar Dance With Me*," Mom interjected.

"Oh, nice," she said. I wasn't convinced she meant it.

Mayuri ran her hand across the hangers dangling on the gold rail and plucked out one dress from the gem-encrusted selection.

My mouth fell open. It was a lavender and gold ombre dress that was beaded from top to toe. The way it glistened and twinkled, catching the light as it moved, was awesome. She passed it to Mom and pointed to a changing room. There was an attendant at the door who opened it for us. She didn't smile.

A few minutes later, I stepped back outside. Mayuri looked at me and the subtle tension that had been etched on her face seemed to lift.

"Oh, wow," she exclaimed as though she was surprised I could look that good. "Jaw-dropping!"

I thought it was a bit odd that she was praising her own dress but I smiled and said "Thank you" just in case she was complimenting me.

Mayuri adjusted my hem. The length at the back was good – not so long that it would catch under my feet. I did a little twirl in front of the mirror. "The off-shoulder style is so pretty," Mayuri muttered to her assistant.

The look on Mom's face told me she didn't agree, but she was never going to tell Mayuri Jain that she would have preferred a more modest neckline.

"It's beautiful. Thank you so much, ma'am," Mom said. I pretended I didn't hear that.

Mayuri shouted out to another assistant, a young man, who scuttled over with a tape measure. She took some measurements and then asked me to change back into my civilian clothing.

I'd expected this unique experience to continue for a

little longer but we were ushered out as quickly as we'd been welcomed in.

"Thank you ever so much," Mom said to Mayuri as we were shown the exit. Perhaps Mayuri didn't hear because she didn't respond, turning instead to the boy who had just walked in.

"Chintu!" I cried out as I realized who he was.

He looked at me and smiled as though he was a superstar and I was a hardcore fan.

"That was awkward," I giggled as we left the fabulous room.

"Hmmm, she was a bit rude," said Mom, taking her phone out of her bag. "Let me just 'check in' to Blockbuster Studios on Facebook."

"Do people actually do that?" I asked.

"Yes, they do," she retorted.

I was just about to inform Mom that only ancient people "checked in" on Facebook when I spotted a familiar figure – or rather two familiar figures – out of the corner of my eye.

"I tell you, I'm not doing it, Dad! Tell Mom I've made up my mind. It's final!"

Monica was clearly not happy with something her parents were asking her to do. She was frowning, but she still looked amazing with her glowing skin and a poker straight bob that swished as she walked.

Shashi was wearing bootcut denim jeans, a matching denim jacket, white snakeskin shoes and a huge pair of gold-rimmed sunglasses. I looked intently at his face but barely recognized him. I had seen quite a few of the superhit movies he had starred in, but he looked pretty different now. He'd lost a fair bit of hair and had gained a pot belly instead.

They walked straight past us as though we were invisible. To say I felt insignificant would be an understatement. I thought Monica might have recognized me. *You know – I'm the girl you gave 8/10 to...*

Mom was taking photos of their backs as they walked off. I didn't know whether to laugh or grab the phone off her.

But I was star-struck too. I'd finally seen some famous people in real life! And in that moment, I knew for sure that I didn't just want to see them – I wanted to *be* one.

Ever since I had been introduced to Bollywood movies, mainly by Daadi and Mom, I'd been hooked. The songs, the dances, the costumes, the escapism they offered had me enchanted. I knew for sure that I wanted to be a Bollywood film star when I grew up. In a country with more than a billion people, the vast majority of whom were movie fans, I guess that wasn't an unusual life goal. But while it was totally out of reach for millions and millions of people, thanks to the platform that Dance Starz could give me, I could almost smell it, touch it, feel it...

Now it was within my grasp, I couldn't let it go.

TAKE FOUR

"Come, one more practice."

"No!" I asserted, pausing the TV and sitting bolt upright. "I told you yesterday, I am *not* rehearsing any more. What is this? Military school?"

Mom crossed her arms and glared at me.

"I know the routine inside out, upside down and back to front," I yelled. "My feet hurt, my legs hurt, my head hurts!"

It was the day of the Dance Starz final and tensions were running high.

"Leave her alone, Shanta," ordered Daadi. "What difference will one more rehearsal make? You're just making her nervous."

"Yes, Mom. Listen to your elders. All I've done for two weeks is dance!"

Mom huffed at being outvoted and quietly carried on tidying around me. She was extra fast at tidying when she was nervous.

Daadi was right. I hadn't done anything since the dress fitting other than dance practice. For half an hour before school, every single day after school, and on both weekends, all I had done was dance. Even while I was sleeping, I could hear *Ek Baar Dance With Me* playing in my head. I didn't want one of my favorite songs to become my worst!

I sighed. At least my finals had taken place before the wild card show. How did star kids manage fame, films and studies?

Besides dance, the only other thing I seemed to do was discreetly check social media and look up my name to see what was being said about me. It seemed I was the second favorite to win the contest – behind Chintu, of course.

I was feeling the heat, no doubt about it. When I first dipped my toe into the Dance Starz waters, I hadn't been that bothered about winning, mostly because I was sure I wouldn't. Now that every single person I knew, including my family and school, were counting on me, I felt scared. Scared of disappointing them. And scared of disappointing myself too.

Chintu was the contestant I had backed all the way from his first audition a few months before to that day in May when he'd won a place in the final. Now that I was up against him, it was awkward to say the least.

But the time for rehearsing was over. This was it.

"Good luck, sweetheart!" Dad said thirty minutes

later. He kissed my forehead as Mom and I rushed into Uncle Manoj's car.

Zara was jumping up and down on the doorstep. "See you there, Bela!" she said eagerly. "I'm going to wear my 'I Back Bela' T-shirt!"

"Me too!" said Daadi. She grabbed Zara's hand and they did a little Mexican wave for me. That helped to melt a little of my tension away. I was trying hard to appear carefree and relaxed when I was anything but.

*

"Gosh, so many people here," said Mom as we pulled into Blockbuster Studios. Predictably, she pulled out her phone to "check in" on Facebook again.

There were loads more ushers this time around, all dressed in navy pants and polo shirts with white badges saying "STAFF." We were led inside to line up for our backstage access passes and to go through security checks.

I'd never been to a live event before, so to be backstage and be given a pass to the Green Room felt really special. I took a photo of my pass and sent it to my friends and Reuben.

"Isn't she the girl who almost lost her leg in an

accident?" Mom asked me, pointing at one of the contestants.

I nodded, pushing Mom's hand down. I didn't want Iqra, who had spent several months in a wheelchair after the accident, to think we were talking about her.

There were some pretty incredible dancers there and they all seemed to know each other. Again, I worried that they would feel I hadn't earned my place.

A roar of applause made me turn back towards the door. Chintu was making an entrance with a series of back flips. Onlookers clapped and cheered.

"He loves being the center of attention, that boy," whispered Mom.

"Yeah. He's so good at it as well," I replied.

Chintu was wearing shades and a silver blazer, jeans and white canvas shoes. He was literally a star in the making. He had the larger-than-life personality to go with the larger-than-life dance skills.

"He won't win though," declared Mom. "He's an acrobat, not a dancer."

I shook my head. What did Mom know? The whole country was backing him. When it came to dance, though, Mom wasn't usually wrong. I reminded myself that she thought I had earned my spot in the final, even if no one else did.

It wasn't long before we were in the Green Room. As luxurious as it was with its oak flooring and opulent emerald-colored sofas, I barely had time to unwind before being whisked into a final dress fitting and a health and safety briefing.

I was trying to take it all in but my mind kept wandering. I was imagining what would happen if I got stage fright. One of the girls had gotten it at a school play the year before. I had felt so bad for her. She had been mortified. What if I froze and couldn't move?

In the meantime, Mom had gone to collect my dress from one of Mayuri Jain's on-site tailors as it had needed a little tightening at the waist. She zipped me into it when she returned. It fit me like a glove.

The hair and makeup team then launched into action. A friendly lady with a hijab got to work on my face. She complimented me on my high cheek bones which I told her I had inherited from my daadi.

As soon as she had dabbed powder on my forehead to stop any shine, a guy took over to style my hair. He tugged and pulled at my hair and I tried not to grimace. It felt more like a factory production line than a pampering experience. This was the first time I had had professional hair and makeup done and I decided I preferred it when Priyanka did me up.

Mom kept a close eye on me, happily snapping photos of all the action on her phone. But she turned very serious when we were informed by a production assistant that it was time for the dress rehearsal.

"I thought we'd get time for a practice together before this," she complained as she was told to head to the main hall.

I put my hand on her arm. "Chill, Mom," I said, even though I felt like freaking out. "I was practicing in my head while the guy was doing my hair."

"Not the same," Mom moaned as she gave me a kiss and then followed the adults into the auditorium. I composed myself with some positive thoughts and joined the contestants backstage to listen for instructions.

We were separated from the main stage by a big black curtain, and while some of the other contestants were peeking through to check out the competition while the dress rehearsal was in progress, I kept my gaze firmly on my side of the room. I knew that if I saw a spectacular performance, it would fill me with insecurities about my own – and it was too late to change my routine.

"Focus on yourself, Bela," I said softly, hearing a huge roar of applause from the audience. Of course it was Chintu entertaining the onlookers. Only he could get cheers that loud.

My heart was thumping a little when it was time for me to take the stage. But the nerves soon dissipated when loud screeching and crackling noises from the speakers drowned out the music of *Ek Baar Dance With Me*.

I kept waiting for the annoying din to disappear, but it didn't. The sound assistants ran around frantically, one of them almost knocking into me as I bent my knees and stretched my arms out, ready for action. I stopped to let them pass.

I spotted Mom. Her arms were folded tightly and she looked cross. By the time they had sorted out the issue, it was time for the next contestant's rehearsal. I slipped away quietly, partly relieved and partly irritated.

One by one, we were sent through an exit door to an outside space where TV cameras were waiting for us. They were filming for the build-up to the show and asking us one question each. I was asked: "Where do you see yourself after this show?"

I could only think of one answer. "Bollywood," I said softly.

By then, I felt like I was in a tailspin. I realized that even to be nervous you needed some energy, and mine was dipping fast.

I wanted to talk to Mom but another contestant told me that chaperones were to stay in the main hall until the end of the show.

I felt hot and my mouth was dry so I took a glass of juice from the refreshment table. I considered a cookie too but really didn't think I would be able to eat it.

Final sound checks were being carried out. The technicians looked worried. They clearly didn't want a repeat of what happened during my dress rehearsal. I tugged at the neckline of my lavender and gold ombre dress to make sure it sat correctly around my shoulders and then stood in line behind the curtain.

We had arrived at the moment of truth. All the other contenders seemed so much more relaxed than me, whispering and giving each other fist bumps. I, meanwhile, felt completely alone. I was sure I was going to cry, or would I be sick? The more I thought about the show being aired in real time, the worse I felt.

The sight of Monica and her famous mom, Malaika Rani, who was looking very glamorous with her heavy makeup, huge eyelashes and flashy diamond rings, distracted me. Monica, I'd learned during the course of the afternoon, wouldn't be on the judging panel. I'd been super relieved to hear that! Instead, she would be presenting the award to the winner at the end of the show.

Malaika introduced Monica to the senior production

staff and then took her over to the waiting media.
She seemed really keen to push her daughter into the
limelight. Malaika's hand on Monica's back as she edged
her towards the cameras was a dead giveaway!

I steeled myself. I had to do justice to my talent. I had
to do justice to my mom's talent. I wanted everyone to
know how good she was, how dedicated she was. I held
onto this thought, knowing it would help me.

"You'll be on fourth, Bela," said an assistant. "Keep
looking at that screen – your name will flash green and
then, as soon as the person on stage is done, your name
will be announced and you'll go on. I'll be here to prompt
you anyway."

I nodded. I wiped my sweaty hands on my beaded
dress as I watched the performances on the screen.

Iqra was called on first. She received a standing
ovation from the crowd before she even moved a muscle.
Her story – of being hit by a car in a road traffic accident
and having her leg crushed to the point of nearly losing
it – had really struck a chord with viewers. Some of the
nasty tabloid newspapers and websites had said she'd
used the sympathy card to get so far but I felt that that
was harsh.

She moved beautifully to a song that was maybe as
old as my daadi. It was from a movie about a young lady

who had to dance outside train stations to earn money. Iqra got the sad expressions totally right. I could tell she had a very slight limp, but that didn't take away from her performance. It made you realize how incredible she was.

The tempo and atmosphere changed completely when Chintu performed. As expected, he covered more of the stage than anybody else with his sequences of flips, cartwheels and acrobatics. I wasn't sure if I imagined it, but Chintu seemed to get less applause than Iqra this time round. I wondered if some people felt that they had already seen everything he could do.

Mithu, the body popper, was next. The spectators clapped along with his incredible routine. I had no idea how he managed to "glitch" to make his body look robotic, and wave and glide with such ease.

I must have lost track of the running order because suddenly the assistant was nudging me and pointing to the screen where my name was flashing. Panic flooded my body. I was momentarily paralyzed.

"Breathe," I told myself. I took in as much air as I could before stepping through the black velvet curtains.

The stage felt unfamiliar and harsh. This was nothing like being in Mom's dance hall. The glass floor was cold. The pin-drop silence just before the music began was deafening. I tried to seek out my family – or a single familiar face – but the lights were blinding.

I did the only thing I knew how: I immersed myself in my art.

First, the Namaskaram – something Mom had taught me to do before and after every performance. With knees bent, and feet pointing outwards, I bent down to the floor to touch Mother Earth with my fingertips, asking her permission to stamp on her during the dance. Standing up, I touched my eyes with my fingertips, joined my hands and then raised them above my head, giving thanks to God. Lowering them to my head, I paid respect to my teacher, my mom. Finally, I brought them to rest in front of my chest, paying respect to the audience.

I was now ready to begin.

Silence. It felt like an eternity before I was rescued by the first few beats of the music. Thankfully, the familiarity of the tune stopped my heart from pounding out of my chest.

I closed my eyes and slowly raised my arm. A calmness came over me as I tapped the floor with my right heel, then stretched my arms out to the sides, pointing my fingers. I didn't even need to think about what I was doing. It came as naturally to me as walking, sleeping, breathing.

I opened my eyes and surveyed the crowd as I moved my head from side to side and glided effortlessly across the stage with tiny, precise movements of my feet. I could hear some gasps from the audience. Mom said it looked like I was floating on water when I moved like that. Is that what they thought too?

The music picked up pace and was suddenly blaring so loud that the stage started vibrating under my feet. A dress rehearsal would have made it feel more familiar but I told myself I just had to adjust. I was guided by the music, and the adrenaline began to make me feel alive. I was now in the flow, using my face to express feelings of sadness and happiness according to the lyrics. My hips swayed freely as I shifted my balance from one foot to the other.

As the chorus pitched in, it was time to showcase my Bollywood moves. If the onlookers had been captivated by my Bharatanatyam skills, they were now invigorated and involved. Some were tapping along, others were singing. That was the point I really let go, using their energy to fuel my performance.

I imagined Mom standing before me, willing me to get each step right: from how high I lifted my hands to where my elbows were in relation to my shoulders, to how quickly I turned.

A series of energetic leaps followed by a dramatic planned fall brought my performance to an end. I suddenly found myself standing up and doing the Namaskaram again to conclude my routine.

As the last notes of the song died out, the crowd erupted. There was so much noise – applause, screaming, shouting, whistling – that there was no way of telling if my family were cheering my name.

"Thank you to our wild card – *Belaaaaaa!*" shouted Raman Sood, a cue for me to vacate the stage.

Part of me wanted to stay there forever and part of me wanted to run away. Would I ever get over it if I didn't even make it to the final three?

A series of high-fives, pats on the back and big smiles by some of the crew members backstage made me think that perhaps I hadn't done so badly after all. Somehow, I still couldn't stop myself from trembling as the remaining acts did their best to win the audience over.

Half an hour later, as I lined up behind the curtain alongside the other contestants ready to go back on stage to be given the final verdict, I felt waves of panic wash over me. People in the crowd were screaming out the names of some of the participants. I couldn't make my name out at all.

I wanted it to be over with. I wanted to go home.

Now, stood there on stage, we had arrived at the defining moment. The moment the audience would pass judgment on us.

It was so daunting, but at the same time, a complete blur – like a dream playing out. I could hear names being announced but it felt like I was frozen in time.

The wild screams of the onlookers suddenly snapped me out of my daze. The stage had all but emptied and there was just myself, Chintu and Grunge Girl Geeta, a street dancer from Delhi, standing alongside Raman Sood.

I hadn't expected Geeta to do so well. She was a brilliant dancer, and so trendy with her baggy pants worn low, but the media hadn't shone a spotlight on her. Turns out she was a dark horse. Could she win the race?

The lights were dimmed low and I suddenly spotted Zara and Daadi waving wildly at me in their "I Back Bela" T-shirts. I was overjoyed to see them. Being alongside Chintu and Grunge Girl Geeta in the final three was an honor. Losing from here would be fine, I consoled myself. I had exceeded all my expectations already.

I closed my eyes as Raman prepared to announce the name of the person in third place. I took a deep breath and planned my gracious exit from the stage.

"Grunge Girl Geeta!"

I let out a long, disbelieving breath. Geeta smiled and blew kisses to the raucous audience before moonwalking off the stage.

Somehow, it was me versus Chintu. Was this some crazy plot twist? Or the Universe playing a joke on me? Maybe Mom had forced this scenario to happen with her visits to the astrologist?

Okay, so I'd come second then. Not too bad. I felt like I had done enough to make my family proud. I didn't even close my eyes this time. I had accepted my fate. I waited.

"And the winner of the Dance Starz final is…"

I thought I was fine, but the dramatic pause was killing me. Time was playing tricks on me as each second felt like an hour. I focused on my sparkly ballerina pumps to stop myself from crumbling under the weight of tension I was feeling. Could the whole country see me quivering like a leaf?

I could hear people chanting. Some were yelling "Bela." Most were screaming for Chintu. Even their voices seemed warped, as though they were in another dimension.

And then, suddenly, like a bolt from the blue, I heard…

"BELA!!!"

My legs gave way from under me. Gold-colored tinsel rained down on me. There was a roar of applause from the audience which felt like a giant wave crashing down around me.

I couldn't believe it. I had won!

I was helped back up by Raman Sood as Chintu waved goodbye to the audience, their cheers nearly raising the roof.

I don't remember exactly what happened next. My mind felt numb.

Some judges spoke. Shashi Kumar announced that I had won a scholarship to the Bollywood Academy from September, the start of the following school year.

At one point, Monica walked onto the stage and stood beside her dad to present me with my award. She handed it to me while aiming her smile at the photographers lined up ahead of us.

"So, Bela, a huge congratulations," said Raman Sood. "What a performance!" He raised his hands to the audience, encouraging them to clap louder. "You were an outsider in this race. You won the wild card show and beat the nation's favorite – Chintu – to win the whole competition *and* the scholarship to the esteemed Bollywood Academy. What a story! How did you do it?"

I was dumbstruck at winning and at beating such incredible competitors. There was a pause as I tried to piece together some words. If I had dared to believe I could win, I would have prepared a victory speech!

My heart was pounding so hard, I was sure everybody could hear it. Raman pointed his microphone at me, looking on, waiting.

"Ummm, I guess it was down to my mom. She's my dance teacher," I said. Even though I had spoken softly, my voice boomed around the stadium. "Mom taught me everything I know...um...and I've been lucky to have a family that has always supported me. I wanted to make them proud, so I focused really hard."

I could hear Reuben and Dad screaming crazily for me. Hearing familiar voices in such an unfamiliar setting helped calm my nerves. I hadn't prepared a speech but I suddenly knew what I wanted to say.

"Ordinary people like us don't get the chance to perform on TV. We don't know anybody in show business...so, yeah...it's almost impossible. I hope other girls like me will believe that they can do it as well. I never thought I could win. I'm so happy Dance Starz gave me a chance. I can't believe I've won a place at the Bollywood Academy!"

Monica, who had been smiling, glanced in my

direction. It was the first time I had seen her look straight at me and I really wasn't sure I liked the expression on her face when she did.

TAKE FIVE

My eyes were red from crying. It was the moment I'd been dreading for eight weeks, ever since winning the show back in July. It was time to say goodbye to my family.

I'd never even been away from my parents for a week. Maybe a few nights when I went to stay with Naani, my maternal grandma. And of course the odd night for sleepovers with my friends.

Ever since we had caught Zara crying silently in her room one night the week before, she had been sleeping with me or my parents.

Daadi had been tearful too. After all her exuberant support, the closer we had gotten to D-Day, the more serious she had become. Daadi had been giving me advice and words of wisdom at every opportunity. She had told me to keep my head down, focus on what I needed to do and keep away from unnecessary drama. I had promised I would. I knew Daadi was going to miss me. Who would she watch all those Bollywood movies with now?

Mom bid farewell to me at the house. She couldn't

come to the Academy to drop me off as it was Saturday and that meant dance classes. Although Mom didn't cry in front of me, she ran back into the house as soon as I had stepped outside. Zara was sobbing so much that Daadi had to take her to the ice cream parlor just before we left. Strangely, though, I was most emotional at Reuben's hug. He hadn't hugged me for a long time now and it really made me realize how much I missed my big brother. I broke away first and quickly got into Uncle Manoj's car, which was waiting in the alleyway outside.

"You okay, Bela?" asked Dad from the passenger seat. He didn't turn to look at me. Maybe he was feeling emotional too.

Mom and Dad had asked me the night before if I was sure I wanted to join the Academy. I had no doubts about that – it was a dream come true. I just wished it didn't mean leaving home.

"You're only two hours away," he added, trying to sound cheerful. "Including the short ferry crossing."

"I can pick you up whenever you want to come home," chipped in Uncle Manoj. "It's no problem."

"You know some of the Academy kids come from abroad?" said Dad. They'd been telling me this all summer and, yes, it was probably true, but it didn't make me feel any better.

Each time I thought about not being able to see my family for weeks at a time, I felt a sense of dread. I'd hardly been gone an hour and I was missing them already! And I wasn't even ready to start thinking of my friends. Would they forget about me? The thought was too much to bear.

I just wanted this journey to be over with. The longer it took, the more time I had to dwell on it. Luckily, the roads became clearer and clearer the further we got from Chandivali. Soon, we arrived at Mumbai's famous arch-monument, the Gateway of India, and waited for our turn to drive onto the ferry that would take us to Kohinoor Island and the Bollywood Academy.

I had visited a couple of Mumbai's other islands during vacations to see their ancient caves and popular beaches but I had never been to Kohinoor Island. It hadn't really been known for anything other than fishermen before the Academy had been built. Along with paddy farmers, fishermen made up the bulk of the 1,500 inhabitants.

The thought of being separated from everything I had ever known by an expanse of water was making me extra nervous. It wasn't like Dad could really drive to me in the middle of the night if I needed him, now could he?

Once aboard the ferry, I must have dozed off for

half an hour or so in the back seat because the next thing I knew, we were off the sea vessel and back on dry land. Ours was the only car for miles around. It felt like we were in a different country. There was greenery everywhere. Fields and fields of green. Not a person in sight.

And then, I saw it.

It looked like a lavish movie set. At the end of a winding road, at the top of a smallish hill with rolling fields all around, stood big gold metal gates with the initials B and A engraved into them in fancy scroll-like letters. Through the gaps in the gates, I could see the most incredible, modernistic building.

"Wow!" exclaimed Uncle Manoj. "It looks like a vacation resort. BA. Bollywood Academy!"

"That is super impressive," agreed Dad. "What do you think, Bela?"

It really did look impressive – even more so than the photos I had seen on the website. In real life, you got to see the full scale and size of the institution. It was both thrilling and terrifying at the same time.

We drove into the visitor parking lot and pulled up. We were literally in the middle of nowhere but the building was sprawling. It was like nothing I had ever seen. Most marble buildings in India had intricate carvings, but this was different. The Academy was built entirely out of marble but it was ultra-modern with clean lines and sharp edges and lots of glass. And it looked spotless. The thought of what lay within the walls and how I would cope alone had my nerves jangling.

Dad obviously sensed my fear. "Look, Bela, nothing has to be forever. If you don't like it, you can leave. As your mom says, just give it a go," he said. "This is an amazing opportunity. You don't want regrets in the future."

I nodded. Knowing that it wasn't a one-way street made it sound not quite so bad.

Uncle Manoj and Dad wheeled my suitcases up the path, past the beautiful fountains and floral border displays on either side. A gardener was tending to the immaculately cut hedges. The edges were so square, they looked artificial.

"It's like a modern palace," said Manoj. "I'm going to take photos to show Rimpi."

The huge glass doors opened automatically as we approached the reception area. As expected, no expense had been spared. The marble floors and gold-flecked tiles on the walls were gleaming.

The receptionist, wearing a cream and navy silk saree with gold border and a BA badge, took my name and told me that the Principal, Mrs. Arora, would be down to greet me.

My welcome letter mentioned that only grade 7 students and new starters would arrive that day. Grades 8-13 would start arriving mid-week. I wondered if I was the only new eighth grader. They must have all established their friendship groups the year before. Would I be known as the new girl? Would I make friends? It was daunting.

I was looking at a gold plaque on the wall with the BA emblem and the words "We hone your talent so you can shine like a star" etched on it, when a small, slightly round woman with a familiar face walked in. She stretched her hand out and spoke in Hindi, perhaps assuming Dad and Uncle Manoj didn't speak English.

"Good afternoon, madam," said Dad, in his finest accent. "I recognize you from the wild card show. You were on the judging panel." I recognized her too, although she looked shorter in real life.

"Oh yes, hello, Mr. Khanna. Nice to meet you. As you know, I'm Mrs. Arora. Welcome to the Bollywood Academy!"

"BA!" said Uncle Manoj, joyous to share the fact that he knew what it stood for.

"Indeed," she smiled. "We assure you we will take

good care of your daughter," she told Dad. "I was so happy when Bela won Dance Starz. Reinventing such a popular song like *Ek Baar Dance With Me* was risky but it really paid off. Personally, I was glad an accomplished Bollywood dancer would be joining us."

I smiled shyly at her. So many people had told me following my victory that, although they were happy I had won, they had been supporting Chintu. But Mrs. Arora had a point – perhaps my dance skills would be more valuable here. In any case, I hoped Chintu would come back and win the next season.

For now, it was time to say goodbye to Dad and Uncle Manoj. Dad welled up when he gave me a hug and, somehow, I managed to keep it all in. But as soon as I saw Uncle Manoj's car drive off, it hit me. Mrs. Arora gave me some tissues. I guess she must have seen that scenario a few times before.

Once I had regained my composure, I followed Mrs. Arora, while a porter trailed behind us with my bags. I really wasn't used to this kind of service! We walked through three long corridors, all featuring Bollywood film posters from the 70s, 80s and 90s. The floors were clinically clean. I hoped my slightly worn shoes weren't leaving scuff marks.

After going up in two different elevators, and then

over a glass bridge that had me feeling giddy, a sign that said "Female Dorms" assured me I had arrived.

"This is your room, Bela," Mrs. Arora said, opening door 987.

I was delighted to see a beautiful, spacious room, not the cramped little dorm I had feared where I wouldn't be able to dance. There were two single beds with ample twirling space between them, two bedside cabinets, two study desks and another door that had a sign saying "Bathroom."

One of the beds was unmade and already had clothes scattered on it.

"Which bed is mine?" I asked stupidly.

"The empty one," Mrs. Arora laughed. "The other one belongs to your roommate, Sophie."

"Oh," I said. I was surprised. I thought the eighth graders weren't coming back until the following week.

"Sophie's an international student," Mrs. Arora elaborated. "She's been here all summer."

I nodded. That made sense. It also made me feel bad for her. I couldn't imagine spending all summer without my family.

Mrs. Arora showed me how to operate the controls to the air conditioning. I couldn't believe that I had AC in my bedroom. Nobody in my neighborhood had AC in their homes, let alone in a kid's bedroom!

"What happens when the electricity goes off?" I asked.

She chuckled. "We don't lose electricity here," Mrs. Arora informed me. "All of our energy is generated by the solar glass panels on the roof or the wind turbines. Look, you can see them from your window."

Mrs. Arora pointed to the three-pronged "trees" lined up along the far side of one of the lawns. I'd seen photos of modern windmills in a geography lesson but never in real life. The Academy was state-of-the-art in every way.

The sound of the bathroom door handle turning interrupted my thoughts.

"Hi!" said the girl who emerged. She was wearing a bath robe and had a towel wrapped neatly around her head. The first thing I noticed was that she didn't look Indian. I wasn't sure why that surprised me.

"I'm Sophie," she proclaimed. I was taken aback at her confidence and presence. She seemed friendly and genuine. I was glad.

"Hi," I replied.

"This is Bela," said Mrs. Arora, helping me out a little. "She's your new roommate. I hope you get on with her as well as you did with Jaymini. It was a shame to see her leave."

I wondered who Jaymini was and why she had left.

"Right, I'll leave you girls to get to know each other. There's still three whole days before the other pupils come back. Make the most of the quiet!"

I thanked Mrs. Arora and then started unzipping my huge, slightly tattered suitcase.

"I couldn't believe it when they told me I was sharing with you," revealed Sophie joyfully. I realized that she spoke with a proper American accent, not the fake American twang so many Bollywood actresses had.

"Really?" I asked.

"I watched the Dance Starz final and was super happy when you won," she went on. "Even though I had no idea we would be roomies."

"Thanks," I said. For some reason, I couldn't get more than one word out at a time. I unpacked some of my clothes and then spotted my fluffy unicorn wrapped in a T-shirt. I discreetly slipped it out of the suitcase and hid it under my pillow. I didn't want Sophie to think I was a baby.

"Your dancing is out of this world!" Sophie declared, her accent sounding more pronounced the more excited she got. "I mean, it's just...even better than actual Bollywood actors!"

I smiled. I decided I was going to like this girl.

"How do you do it?

"I find dance easy," I answered simply. "It's literally like running or walking to me. My mom is a dance teacher so I've done it all my life."

"Wow," said Sophie, pulling the towel off her head and running her fingers through her wet hair. "That's so cool. But you must be naturally good at it. I've been dancing for ages but I don't find it so easy."

"Oh, really?" I said. I wanted to take my shoes off but didn't quite feel comfortable yet. "Where are you from?"

Sophie walked over to the long mirror in between the two closets and combed her hair.

"I'm from Canada. Can't you tell from the accent?"

"Yes, of course," I lied. "I meant... Umm, you don't look Indian."

"I'm half Indian, quarter French and quarter Belgian."

That confused me.

"My mom is Indian – born here but raised in Canada. My dad is white European. Half Belgian and half French."

"So how come you're here? Oops, sorry, I didn't mean it like that," I added, putting a hand over my mouth.

"It's okay. Everyone asks me that question," she replied. "My mom always wanted to be a Bollywood star and I grew up watching movies with her. She asked me when I was six if I wanted to become an actor and I said yes. But what did I know at six?" Sophie laughed again.

I picked up my suitcase and tipped all the contents out onto my bed. Maybe it would be quicker this way.

"Here, let me help," offered Sophie, gently picking up a few items of clothing and placing them neatly to one side.

"But I'm not so sure anymore," she went on.

"What do you mean?"

"Well, the Academy kids are always going for auditions for small parts in TV shows and movies," she explained, waving one of my T-shirts around as she spoke. "But it's always the insider kids who get the roles. It's costing my parents a lot for me to be here and we don't know if it's worth it."

"What are insider kids?" I probed, hesitating a little in case it was a really stupid question.

"Star kids. Ones with moms, dads, family members who are already famous or in the film industry."

"You mean, like Monica?"

Sophie threw her head back and laughed. "Oh my! I mean exactly like Monica! She is literally the definition of insider!" She giggled some more.

"There are others too," she added mysteriously. "Some of them you'd never even know were insiders."

"Huh?"

"They might be kids of script writers or related to film investors. They might not be more talented or better for the role but they still get picked for jobs over us. There's an actual name for it – nepotism. My dad says it happens everywhere but it's really bad in Bollywood."

I thought I understood. At the very least, I knew I wasn't a star kid.

"I like that you're an outsider," Sophie smiled. "My last roomie, Jaymini – she was too. We were besties."

Sophie pointed to a photo on her desk – a picture of her with Jaymini. They were laughing. Jaymini had her tongue out and they were doing the peace "V" sign.

"Where did she go?" I questioned.

"She left. She almost got a really big role last year in a show on Amazon Prime and then, right at the last minute, she got replaced by the daughter of a music producer. I didn't think it was such a big deal but she got really upset and left."

I was sad to hear that. Poor Jaymini.

"I hope you won't do that to me," Sophie smiled. "You're here to stay, right Bela? We can be outsiders together."

I hoped I was there to stay. But I didn't want to be labeled an outsider. I couldn't help the fact that I wasn't

born to someone already in the industry, but my talent
would see me through.

Wouldn't it?

*

I had a fun few days getting to know Sophie and
acquainting myself with the Academy and its awesome
architecture and surroundings. Sophie said she was
happy to act as tour guide and showed me all the must-
see sights, including the Games Room with its foosball
table, pool table, and gaming consoles.

I couldn't believe my eyes when she took me to the
Olympic-sized swimming pool. The walls were entirely
made of glass so that from one side of the pool you could
see the incredible grounds of the Academy and a lot of
Kohinoor Island. And the best part? The glass roof was
retractable!

There were tennis courts, basketball courts, and
soccer and hockey fields too. No wonder Sophie didn't
get bored over the summer. Being a sporty girl, this place
was heaven for her. I felt like I would be spending a lot
of time in the amazing TV room with its 100-inch TV
screen. Throw in Movie Nights, which Sophie told me
took place in an amazing observatory that I was yet to

see, and I was sure this place would suit me fine!

One of the dining hall assistants told us that the Academy had been built on an island to keep the students away from photographers and members of the public who might want to hang around in the hope of seeing star children. That made sense. I had never seen a place with so few people.

For the first couple of days, I felt like I was on vacation. It was weird that this was going to be my school. I called my family several times, giving them live video tours. The "Oooh," "Aaah," "Wow" sounds they made as I walked around, showing them all the amazing facilities, were funny. They even had a chat with Sophie which was nice.

I missed Zara a lot. The first few times I had spoken to her, she had just cried. A day or so later, she had started telling me stuff about her day and asking about mine. Now, she asked to speak to Sophie first!

The time whizzed by so fast that it wasn't long before it was Tuesday evening, the day before school was due to start. Sophie and I had packed our book bags, hung up our uniforms and were making our way downstairs to the cafeteria.

"Oh my goodness," I whispered as we queued for our dinner in the huge dining hall. "It's so busy. It doesn't even feel like the same place!"

Most of the students had been arriving throughout the day. I looked around, expecting to see some famous faces, but I didn't recognize anyone at first. Then I stopped.

"Oh!" I said, louder than I'd intended to. "Who's that?" I pointed at a tall, lanky boy with curly, brownish hair. His cute face looked familiar.

"The guy with the gray jeans?" asked Sophie. "That's Marc Fernandez."

"As in Rocky from *Rescue*?" I was trying not to, but I felt like I was getting star-struck again.

Sophie nodded. "Yeah – he's an insider but one of the nicer ones!" she chuckled. "His aunt is Rita Fernandez."

"The item girl?" I asked, referring to a famous actress who had made her name by appearing in movies just for a hit song rather than a full role.

"Yep!" Sophie confirmed. "Apparently, she doesn't have kids of her own so she dotes on him."

When Marc's debut movie, *Rescue*, was released, I was nine years old. He was the star of the film, a comedy about a kid who gets trapped in a video game. I'd watched it over and over to the point where Daadi had had to hide the DVD!

"He hangs out with all the Rich_Kids_of_Instagram.

Have you seen those accounts?"

I nodded. "When my mom lets me. She is *soooo* strict about phone use. I literally only got a cell after I agreed to enter the wild card show. And I still can't create any social media accounts till I turn thirteen in May!"

We moved to the counter where we chose from a wide variety of dishes. There was pizza, pasta, salads, some Chinese options as well as Indian. I definitely wasn't going to go hungry! I opted for chickpeas and rice, which was nice but nowhere near as good as Mom's. It made me miss her.

After dinner, Sophie went to visit a couple of her friends from her year group. She invited me but I didn't feel comfortable. I felt instead that I needed to prepare for the day ahead. As much as I loved this institution with its world-class facilities, I couldn't help but miss the hustle, bustle and craziness of my ordinary life. It was so carefree and relaxed at home.

There was an etiquette at the Academy that you had to adhere to and I felt acutely aware that I was there on a scholarship. My parents could never in their lifetimes pay the Academy school fees. If they had seen some of the supercars pull up when the bulk of the students arrived that day, they would have been shocked.

I was different. I knew I was. I was nervous about what

the rich "in" kids would think of me: the way I spoke, my dress sense, my family, my home.

But the thought that I was trying to cling on to was that I was there on merit, not because I had been born into a privileged home. I really enjoyed performing. I loved dancing – it was a craft I wanted to perfect. And it was something that bonded me and my mom together. Winning Dance Starz had helped Mom's dance class grow – she had a full class of thirty students now, compared to the ten before I won.

My popularity was rising too. Last time I typed my name into Google, there were pages of mentions. That was mind-boggling to me! I might have been an outsider, but I could sense what life was like on the inside.

I just needed to find a way to break in.

TAKE SIX

According to my printed schedule, my very first class at my new school was History. There were three main departments at the Academy – Drama, Technical, and Music & Dance – but we wouldn't choose our specialties until ninth grade. For now, the only thing that separated us was the homerooms we were put in.

I was in Miss Takkar's homeroom. Sophie was in Mr. Mehta's. We all had to report to our homeroom teachers at the end of each day. I would have loved to be in the same class as Sophie but I had no control over that. I was determined to be on time though, so I set off for the classroom twenty minutes early. But no matter which way I turned, I ended up back at the same huge spiral stairway near the entrance. I knew it was the same stairway because there was a metal statue of somebody important – an old man with a bald head. I followed the sign that said "Reception."

"Sorry, but I need classroom H4," I muttered to the receptionist, holding out my piece of paper. She looked at me as though trying to recall where she might have seen me before. Or perhaps I was imagining it. A lot of people looked at me a little strangely since I had won Dance Starz.

"Hey, hey!" the receptionist said, pointing to the group of boys that were walking past. They stopped.

"Yes, Miss?" said one.

It was Marc, the boy who I had seen in the cafeteria and recognized from *Rescue*. I straightened up and tucked some loose strands of hair behind my ear.

"Are you boys going to Class H4?"

Marc nodded. "Can you please take this young lady with you? She's lost," said the receptionist.

"It's that dancing girl," whispered one of them.

The boys laughed. "Scholarship girl."

I went bright red.

"Ignore them," said Marc, looking embarrassed. He gestured for me to follow them. "What's your name?"

"Bela," I muttered.

"Aah yes," he responded. I wasn't sure what he meant by that.

When we reached the classroom, I stood quietly in line behind them as they discussed a cricket game that had taken place the day before. I noticed how everyone was so immaculately dressed. At my old school, most of the kids would have slightly scuffed shoes that were made good for the first day back. Here, every collar, cuff and toecap was pristine. I had bought new shoes and, of course, the uniform that Dad complained had cost an arm and a leg.

As soon as the door to the classroom opened at 9am on the dot, the boys all rushed to the back of class. I chose a desk on one side of the room where I would be least visible. The room filled up fast. I scanned the faces around me, stopping only when I spotted Monica. Just my luck that she'd be in my class when Sophie wasn't!

Monica was chattering away to her friends and I busied myself organizing my text books. I didn't want her to notice me, maybe because of the piercing look she had given me at the Dance Starz final. What did she make of me winning?

"Okay, everybody," began the teacher, Mr. Ibrahim. "I hope you all had a great summer break." The pupils quieted down. "Before we begin class, I want to introduce you all to our new starters."

Heat rose up my body as a few people turned to look at me. I couldn't make out the whispers.

"Firstly, we have this young man," he said, pointing to a Sikh boy at the front of the class. "Parminder is from the Punjab and tells me he wants to major in cinematography. He was also a top county cricket bowler so we hope he will join the Academy cricket team. Please give him a warm welcome."

Parminder stood up and smiled at everyone. He looked so confident. I was anything *but* when it came to this kind of attention. Put me on stage to dance – no problem. Stand me up to talk to my own class – problem!

"Secondly, I'm very pleased to welcome a young lady who stole the judges' hearts in the final of the TV show Dance Starz!"

I was burning up. I didn't stand. I tried to smile.

"Welcome, Bela!" Mr. Ibrahim clapped loudly. "How have you found the Academy so far?"

"Ummm...well...it's really nice. It's really big..." I was acutely aware that every single person was staring at me. "I got lost finding the classroom today. I kept ending up at the statue."

"Which one? The statue of Harish Kumar?" he asked.

"Not sure, sir. It was the statue of the bald man, by the stairs."

Several students burst out laughing. "The bald man! She actually said that!"

I gulped, not sure why they were snickering.

"Excuse me, sir," said Monica, in a voice dripping with disdain. "Maybe you can explain to her that that 'bald man' is my great grandfather!"

I froze. My face flushed so hard that I thought I might

spontaneously combust. Beads of sweat formed around
my hairline.

"Bela, the statue is of Mr. Harish Kumar, one of the
founding fathers of Bollywood cinema – the father of
Bhushan Kumar, the grandfather of Shashi Kumar, and
the great grandfather of Monica."

I nodded. Lesson learned.

"That's what you get when you encourage outsiders to
join the Academy," hissed Monica.

"That's enough, Monica!" reprimanded Mr. Ibrahim.
"Not everybody knows everything – including yourself.
That is why we're here: to learn. I won't tolerate any kind
of rudeness."

She slumped back in her chair and gave Mr. Ibrahim a
stare as he got his lesson underway.

I was totally taken aback. Why would she say such a
mean thing? I desperately wanted the lesson to end so
I could just get out of there and organize my feelings. I
tried so hard to focus on what Mr. Ibrahim was trying
to teach us. I wrote down some key dates he mentioned
although my mind didn't connect them to anything. I
was in a bit of a haze and beyond glad when the bell rang.

"You have *no idea* how embarrassing that was," I told
Sophie the minute she walked back into our room at the
end of the school day.

She looked puzzled but took a seat, backpack in her lap, until I was done ranting. It took a while.

"Oh, Bela," Sophie sighed. "You really don't want to get on the wrong side of Monica. She's Shashi Kumar's daughter. He does own this place after all."

"I'm not even trying to make this into a thing," I said defensively. "I mean, how am I supposed to know her great great grandfather?"

"Great grandfather," Sophie corrected.

"Yeah, whatever. I mean, does she know who my great grandfather was?"

Sophie fell back on the bed and started laughing. "That's true, Bela, but it's hardly the same thing!"

I managed a smile. I suppose I could see the funny side of it.

"Her great grandfather is really famous. But yeah, why should you know all the names of the old actors in Bollywood? By the way, we covered the history of Bollywood in seventh grade – the year you missed."

"Well, there you go," I said. "I missed that class!"

"If you hadn't called him 'the bald guy,' it might not have made her so mad."

I looked at Sophie and I saw it. It was a comedy of errors. I flopped back on my bed and we laughed and laughed until our sides ached.

*

"Out!"

The PE teacher, Mr. Khan, smiled at me. "It's okay, Bela. If it's the first time you've played tennis, I don't expect you to be able to rally."

I tried to smile back but was acutely aware that I'd just shown myself up. I'd never even seen a real-life tennis court, let alone played on one. All my class members were sitting on the white wooden benches on one side of the immaculate lawn tennis courts from where you could see the lush landscape of Kohinoor Island all the way down to the sea. They clapped politely as I handed my racket to another student called Deepa who was also in my homeroom.

I went to grab my towel from my bag as Deepa and Mr. Khan started hitting the ball back and forth over the net. I saw Miss Takkar entering the court.

My homeroom tutor, known as Miss T for short, was also Head of Drama. She was strict, with a zero tolerance approach to pretty much everything. I had only been there for three weeks but I'd already sussed that she was a real stickler for the rules.

"Sorry to interrupt, Mr. Khan," began Miss T, sipping water from a bottle. It was a humid afternoon. "Can I please have a quiet word with Bela Khanna?"

What have I done? I wondered. Had she seen my pathetic attempt at trying to get the ball over the net? I walked over and we went inside the Sports Arena to catch some shade.

"Mr. Shashi Kumar would like to invite you to an audition next week, Bela," stated Miss Takkar.

"Oh!" I squeaked. I couldn't believe Shashi Kumar had sent her to talk to me! Sophie had mentioned an upcoming audition but I hadn't planned on going for one so soon.

"We emailed the details to all students last week and we gather you didn't apply," said Miss Takkar, no doubt wanting to hear why. While auditions were not compulsory, the Academy encouraged us to do as many as we possibly could. The more auditions we did, the more jobs the Academy could boast of.

"Sorry, Miss. I didn't think I was ready yet..." I mumbled.

"Of course you're ready!" said Miss Takkar, trying to motivate me. "The experience alone is worth it. Check your email and we look forward to seeing you at 4pm on the day."

The first thing I did when I got back to my room at the end of class was take the email out of my trash folder.

I quickly gleaned the following facts: the audition was for a movie titled *Mystery* to be produced by Malica Productions; shooting was already 90% complete but they needed two people for some key scenes: one girl aged 11-13 with good acting skills, any height, and one boy aged 11-14, 5ft 9in or above, with good Hindi, stunt experience and good general acting skills; time and location: September 22, 4pm, Performance Hall.

"A personal invitation from *the* Shashi Kumar?" Reuben said when I called home a few minutes later. "That means he wants you for the role, otherwise they would never have bothered finding you to audition."

Mom was delighted and said she would go to the mandir to pray, while Dad thought it would boost my confidence when it came to job interviews when I was older. My heart fluttered with excitement at the prospect of being on the silver screen, even though my expectation of scoring the part was low.

I tried to convince Sophie to audition when she got back to the dorm room but she said she'd already done loads of auditions in seventh grade and never got anywhere. "I might switch to directing when we choose our options next year," she said cheerily. "I think it's easier to crack Bollywood from behind the camera."

I was saddened that she'd all but given up on her

desire to act after just one year.

It turned out that there was no shortage of auditionees. When the day came, a big queue of students snaked outside the Performance Hall. The teachers were sending pupils in one by one. I couldn't see what was happening inside but I calculated that each audition took a total of two minutes.

I overheard one of the boys in front whispering to his friend: "Shashi Kumar is in there!"

The friend replied, "Of course he's in there. Malica Productions is *his* company, duh! It's named after his wife and daughter, Malaika and Monica: Malica."

Uff. I had had no idea, but it seemed obvious now. Shashi Kumar seemed to be everywhere. Did that also mean that Monica would be inside? Maybe auditioning for the same role? Would she even need to audition for a job with her dad?

"Excuse me," I said to the boys. "Do you know what we need to say or do?" It was unlike me to talk spontaneously to strangers but I wanted as much information as possible before I went inside.

One of the boys – the tallest – looked down at me. "You're Bela, right?" he asked.

I smiled, taken aback that he knew who I was.

"I'm Ravi," he said, politely introducing himself. "I

have no idea what we need to do. Just go with the flow."

Talking to Ravi calmed my nerves a little. He was really motivated by this role since it needed stunt experience. Ravi was only in seventh grade but he was a Taekwondo black belt. I was still listening to his story of how he came to be at the Academy when I was told it was my turn.

Inside, facing another panel of judges, I gave my name. It was noted by Academy staff member Jagdish who pointed to where I needed to stand. Jagdish, whose official title was Site Manager, had a small build, and his thick black mustache overwhelmed his small, square face. Sophie told me his nickname was Jolly Jags, but this was ironic. He was known to be curt and abrupt, which was odd considering he was the key contact between the Academy and any external agencies, including film producers and studios.

Jagdish introduced me to the panel members. I didn't recognize any of them except for Shashi Kumar. He was looking at me intently. I'd hoped he would be all "Hey, Bela, the amazing winner of my show!" but he just stared. It was extra weird considering how he'd gone out of his way to get me to audition in the first place!

"Okay, you need to pretend that you think your dog has been kidnapped," Jagdish told me, as though he wanted me in and out fast. "Without using any words, convey your emotions."

I was stumped. I'd never had a pet in my life. I tried to imagine what I would feel and it was not easy at all. I was pretty sure the only emotion I was conveying was confusion. When I was done, Shashi Kumar certainly didn't look as though I had bowled him over.

As I headed out, one of Monica's besties – Amrita, known as A for short – strode in. She was pretty, with very short hair in a style my daadi would have insisted was a "boy cut." Being the daughter of an actor, albeit someone who played more villainous characters, she would have a much better chance of scoring this role. I was certain that this little "take" would end there for me.

"It's all about the experience," Miss Takkar told me the following day during homeroom time. "Auditions build your skills and talent. You may not do so well in one, but it will teach you how to improve for the next one."

I hoped she was right. I had zero hope of landing the part in *Mystery* since I was such a newbie. Maybe Shashi Kumar had asked me to do it so I could get experience of auditions? All my peers seemed to have done at least two in seventh grade.

The wait was due to end soon in any case. The

outcome of the audition was being announced at the end of the day. I wouldn't be there, I decided. I had promised Zara I would video call her at 5pm since it was her 7th birthday. Her friends would be over and I was really looking forward to seeing them all. It made me sad to think I couldn't be there to help plan it. Daadi and I had really gone to town for her previous disco-themed birthday, blowing up balloons and hiding little toys for her around the house.

I was in the middle of my call with Zara, Rimpi and the other neighborhood kids when there was a loud banging on my door.

"Bela! Bela! Open, quick!"

I opened the door and saw Tara, one of Sophie's best friends. She was British – from the East End of London – and she had, I was told, a "Cockney" accent. She also randomly dropped Cockney rhyming slang into her sentences. She'd learned it from her grandfather – a proud East Ender. Dog and bone, meaning phone, was the first one she had tried to teach me.

"Sophie sent me," she puffed, out of breath from running. "She's still in class but she told me to tell you. You got it!"

"Got wha–?"

"What's happening, Bela?" Zara shouted.

"Wow – hold on – let Tara speak!"

I was shaking, but held up my phone so Tara could announce it.

"Bela got the part in *Mystery!*" she yelled into it.

Mom and Daadi rushed over to join the call and it was complete chaos from there on in. Reuben grabbed the tablet and ran off with it. All I could see was a close up of him doing high fives all round. I laughed. I didn't think he would be that bothered!

I promised to call back later and then ran downstairs with Tara.

We pushed open the double doors of the Performance Hall to find Jagdish, Miss T and a group of students chatting. The room fell silent when Tara and I walked in. The students, some of them muttering to each other in hushed tones, filed out of the room under instructions from Jagdish.

"Congratulations, Bela!" Miss Takkar said jovially. I hadn't ever seen her looking so chirpy. "You've won the part!"

Tara was clapping wildly and seemed almost as excited as I was! At that moment, Sophie burst in and literally knocked me down as she grabbed me.

I was stiff with shock. No way was this happening. I'd only been at the Academy for a month. I never thought

I'd get chosen for a part in a real movie!

Jagdish didn't say much and he didn't look particularly impressed. He handed me a letter. "This has all the details. You may need to get yourself an agent. You can speak to Miss Takkar about this. A copy of the letter will be sent to your parents."

I was about to open it when someone tapped me on the shoulder.

"Well done, Bela!" came a boy's voice.

I turned around. It was Ravi, the tall stunt boy. "I got chosen too! I can't believe it." I was happy for him. What a nice surprise that we had both been chosen! He was also clutching a letter.

We were making our way out some twenty minutes later, when Monica – along with A and another friend, Bahnaz, who Sophie and I had nicknamed B – walked in. They completely ignored us.

"Miss," Amrita said to Miss Takkar. She didn't sound happy. "Is it true that the female part went to the winner of Dance Starz because they want to promote the show? To get more people to audition for Season Two?"

I stopped walking. I turned around.

"Of course not!" said Miss Takkar firmly. "The roles were given on merit. Who told you this nonsense? I've already had one group of students complaining."

"Maybe the stunt boy role was given on merit but the female part was definitely chosen to promote the show. Trust me," Monica told Amrita loudly.

Miss Takkar looked sternly at Monica.

"Anyway, it's a really small insignificant role," Monica continued. "Why do you think I didn't audition for it?"

The smile had been well and truly wiped off my face.

Sophie and Tara linked arms with me and ushered me out of the hall. Ravi gave me an uncomfortable goodbye wave as he walked off.

I was deflated. Monica seemed to exist to humiliate me.

The part in *Mystery* might have been a nothing, meaningless role for her, but for me, my friends and my family, it was a big deal.

I wasn't going to let this jumped-up starlet crush my dreams.

TAKE SEVEN

My first day on a real-life set was one I wasn't going to forget for the rest of my life. Yes, I'd read the script and come to realize that mine was a small role, but the fact that I would be immortalized on film was big.

My parents were beyond proud. Mom hadn't stopped buzzing since she'd found out, and even Reuben was showing off, tagging me in pics on his Instagram account. I was shocked and secretly pleased to see he'd written "Bela's brother" on his profile. My classmates all demanded photos of anything and everything to do with #setlife.

We were shooting in some woodland on the west side of Kohinoor Island. The film's director, Xavier, handed me the call sheet and told me that my part in *Mystery* was central to the movie even though I had no dialogue. It was about a girl who went missing, played by me. But because I mysteriously vanished in the opening scene and didn't get discovered until the last, I wouldn't be on set for very long.

"Quality, not quantity," Dad had said.

I'd also been told that I would feature on some of the

movie posters. That was huge!

A really famous movie star would be playing my dad. I'd already planned to tag him on social media when I got my own accounts and I promised Daadi I would get his autograph.

In the month since I'd found out I had won the role, I had managed to get myself an agent, Jaya, and sign an official contract. Apparently my fee was equivalent to six months of Dad's wages! The only downside was that filming was during the October mid-semester break and I wouldn't get to go home for the full week.

"I guess you know that most of the movie has already been shot," Xavier informed me as I scoured the call sheet, not fully understanding all the information. "A lot of your scenes will be filmed today. If we need anything extra, we have tomorrow."

I was listening to Xavier but I couldn't help getting distracted by everything going on around me. There was so much backstage action: the camera operators moving the cameras around on huge platforms with wheels; the multiple lighting technicians; all the people sitting in front of portable computers and screens. I had watched hundreds of Bollywood movies and knew the names of all the actors, most directors, and some producers too. But I had no idea that making a movie involved so many people!

I also didn't realize how long everything took. Three hours later, I was still just sitting on the sidelines. I yawned.

"Stay alert," said Miss Takkar. As the Head of Drama, she was accompanying me since my parents couldn't. She had a wad of test papers to mark and was making steady progress. For me, it was a different story. I had nothing to do. We weren't allowed to use our phones on set unless we were on a break – the Academy had a zero-tolerance policy.

Thankfully, a man with a sleek bob haircut came to the rescue. "You're Bela, I presume," he said cheerily, putting his hand out. I stood up and gave him a handshake.

"I'm Monty," he said. "Your makeup artist."

I smiled, relieved that something was finally happening. He seemed like fun and, for some reason, I felt instantly comfortable with him.

Monty led me toward a trailer and we stepped inside. It was basically a mobile dressing room. There were huge mirrors with lightbulbs all around them, a fluffy fake tiger-skin rug, and lots and lots of makeup. I couldn't wait to tell Priyanka about this – she would be in heaven!

"The only thing is," said Monty as he brushed my hair

up into a bun and secured it to keep it out of my face, "it's not the kind of makeup most girls like."

I was puzzled.

"I've been asked to make you look as though you've been hiding out in the woods on your own for days on end." He grimaced. "*Dahling*, I'm about to make you look as unglamorous as you've ever looked."

I nodded. Not ideal, but that's okay, I thought. All part and parcel of being an actor...until I saw the end result. I mean, I looked like I had jumped into a mud pit. I could have been anyone! *Why did they choose me?* I wondered as I stood in the dark, scary woodland with the lights dimmed low.

It didn't take me long to finish the job. I had to dart around here and there, fall over a few times, scream and run around a bit more.

"Well done, Bela!" said Xavier, as we wrapped up the day's shoot. "Having you on board is great publicity for Dance Starz. Shashi Kumar will be tickled pink."

I looked over at Miss T. She caught my eye but looked away.

Monica was right, after all.

*

At home in Chandivali, barely anyone recognized me as the girl on the *Mystery* posters. Daadi, Zara, Reuben and his friend Mujeeb posed in front of some of the hoardings and sent me pics, but I felt like I had been duped into taking on a stupid job. At the Academy, only the people I was in direct contact with seemed to know anything about the movie. It felt like such an anti-climax.

"You should have checked her role. That's your job!" Mom had shouted down the phone at Jaya. "What do you take 15% commission for?"

Jaya had promptly reminded Mom that we had been paid handsomely for the "small but central part." Mom had had no answer to that – the money had been very good.

I decided to put it down to experience. It may not have been a great one but it hadn't been a terrible one either, especially for a rookie like me who was still settling in.

Mystery did decent business at the box office but nobody was talking about it. They were all talking about something else.

Nepotism.

The same thing Sophie had told me about – the very reason Jaymini had quit the Academy, fed up with coming up short against "insider" kids. There was a sudden and unexpected backlash against it.

An aging actress, Sonia Soni, had just quit the film industry. Her parting shot was a sensational video she posted online claiming that her career was destroyed by the so-called Bollywood mafia – the insiders who made sure that they and their kids always got the best opportunities.

Sonia's video going viral had meant that the hashtags #NepotismInBollywood and #BoycottBullywood had started trending. The film industry's top stars – actors mainly – were getting trolled and ridiculed to the point where they had to turn off the comments sections on their social media accounts. What was once their strength was fast becoming their weakness. It was getting to the point where some film stars were refusing to discuss their family connections in interviews for fear of being mocked.

Mom, though, was loving it. "About time too!" she had said when I called her after my gym class one afternoon.

I wondered what Monica felt about it, but I had barely seen her at school over the past few days. Apparently, she was busy with some modeling gigs. She was there, however, on the day everyone was clamoring around the noticeboard in the Performance Hall.

"Bela!" Tara and Sophie were at the front, beckoning me. I squeezed my way past several students to join them.

"Look!" They both pointed. On gold-colored paper, a notice took pride of place.

WANTED!
Six cast members to star in a Cinema Factory production titled *Jigsaw*. Three girls, three boys. Grades 7 and 8 only. Applicants must have acting and dancing skills. ALSO NEEDED: 12 students to shadow senior technicians on set and gain experience as runners. Shooting will take place from Dec 15 to Feb 28. Pre-release publicity will include *FilmGlitz* photoshoot. Send showreels to Miss Takkar by Nov 22.

There was feverish chatter as people thronged around the poster. Some of the students were buzzing about the technical opportunities. Others were raving about the chance of a photo shoot with *FilmGlitz*, one of the magazines I collected. But the vast majority were drooling at the thought of being in a Cinema Factory production. Cinema Factory was Bollywood's version of Disney – the biggest and most famous production company.

All of those reasons were good enough for me too. But I was particularly interested in this audition because they weren't just looking for one girl; they wanted three. Even if I was up against someone with more experience or connections, there could still be space for me.

"I tell you, looks like it's one for me," said Monica confidently. She looked at her friends. "You guys can apply to shadow the technicians, right?"

They nodded.

Wow, I thought to myself. *She actually wields that much power?* Amrita was the daughter of an actor and Bahnaz was the daughter of a billionaire, apparently. Yet when Monica snapped her fingers, they jumped.

"I'll be sending my showreel tonight," smirked Monica.

Showreel? I didn't even have one. I would have to ask Miss T to help me.

"You mean it's not your dad's movie, Mon?" joked Marc. "You actually have to audition?"

I stifled a laugh.

"Ha ha, Marc," she retorted. "Very funny coming from someone else with connections!" She looked sideways at me before turning to Marc. "Well, I'm sure they want *real* actors for this role, not reality TV people."

"Ooooh," drawled Marc. "Who was that dig aimed at?"

Tara and Sophie jogged me to say something but I didn't want to.

"You know Bela is a bigger star than all of us now, Monica?" said Shamim, Marc's best friend.

I blushed.

"You what?" said Monica.

"Well, she's starred in a movie now. And it's a hit. She's made it."

"Hahahahaha! Call that a movie role?" Monica smirked. "Being coated in mud and mute for a one-minute role doesn't make you a star!"

Her pals roared with laughter.

"It was an acting role, not a modeling assignment," I said, suddenly finding my voice. "And I got it on merit."

Monica and her friends stopped snickering.

"You go, girl!" said Tara. Sophie squeezed my arm in support.

"Time to clear the hall!" shouted Jagdish, appearing from nowhere. He steered everyone towards the doors. "We will be emailing this to all of you. Everyone leave the hall now!"

I'd never been so happy to see Jolly Jags. And I'd never been more determined to work for something I wanted.

Monica might have been able to intimidate her so-called friends into taking a back seat, but there was no way I was going to let her do that to me.

*

Academy classes continued as normal over the next few days but there was an air of tension over who would emerge victorious with a part in *Jigsaw*. Rumor had it that two of the acting roles would be lead roles, and that there was an outdoor shoot scheduled too.

Miss Takkar had arranged for me to put a quick showreel together. I think she realized I didn't have the resources other kids had so she'd persuaded one of the staff technicians to volunteer.

Sophie decided not to audition, even for the technical roles, because there was a big soccer tournament taking place during filming. So, it was just me and Tara.

"Imagine if we both get chosen," I said to Tara on Friday afternoon as we headed to the Performance Hall where Miss T and Jagdish would be making the announcement. "We'd have so much fun. And I'd die to shoot for *FilmGlitz*. That would be so amazing!"

She agreed. "It'd be mother's pearly gate!"

I gave her a sidelong glance.

"Great!" she translated.

We giggled as we entered the hall, wandering over towards the middle of the seating area and settling down.

Marc was sitting in the front row with his friends. Out of the corner of my eye, I noticed Monica walk in with Amrita. Bahnaz followed close behind, clutching her Gucci handbag. Monica made a beeline for the empty seat next to Marc and started chatting away. They were obviously comfortable with each other. I wondered what kind of things they talked about. Perhaps they had mutual friends and family members.

Jagdish and Miss T took their position on the podium in front of us. Jagdish gave us a business-like welcome and promptly informed us that the Academy staff had initially shortlisted twelve students for the acting roles while twenty-four had been shortlisted to shadow the technicians. Cinema Factory had whittled that down to six actors and twelve technicians.

I looked around the room and realized that there were around thirty to forty students there. My shoulders slumped a little as I prepared myself for disappointment.

The names of the students who had been assigned technical roles were read out by Miss Takkar. A and B stood up and high-fived when their names were announced. Monica gave them a thumbs-up.

"Yes!" Tara shouted when her name was read out.
I was so happy for her! But increasingly nervous for
myself.

It was crunch time...

"Now to declare the names of those who have won
acting roles," began Jagdish, smoothing down the sheet
of paper in front of him. "Ajay Banerjee, Deepa Gill,
Shamim Khan and Monica Kumar," he said, looking up.

All the victorious students and some of their friends
screamed and clapped. Monica was getting hugs from
her besties and Ajay and Deepa were congratulating each
other.

Tara looked at me.

"Oh, well," I muttered, playing down my
disappointment.

"But that's only four," said Tara loudly.

"Let me finish!" snapped Jagdish.

"I have announced four names. Which means that the
final two – the ones who will be taking on the lead roles
of Vikram and Saaya – are Marc Fernandez and Bela
Khanna."

Tara let out a scream and grabbed me, hugging me so
tight. I was in a state of disbelief, shaking as I removed
myself from her grip. That was some unexpected turn of
events!

Monica – clearly outraged at the revelation – stood up and walked out, A and B scuttling off after her.

Marc was being hoisted up onto the shoulders of Ajay and Shamim. He made a heart sign with his hands as he smiled at me.

Was I dreaming?

This kind of thing didn't usually happen to ordinary girls from ordinary families like mine.

It was incredible enough to get a scholarship to the Academy.

Getting a role in a real movie seemed like a miracle.

TAKE EIGHT

"I tell you, who does she think she is?"

I strained to hear more clearly. It was definitely Monica. Nobody else I knew said "I tell you" at the start of practically every sentence.

"I mean, first dissing my modeling career and implying I get jobs I don't deserve," she started.

"Exactly! That's just rude," said another girl who I assumed was Amrita.

I held my breath. Did they know I could hear them?

"Then calling my great grandfather bald! That's just disrespectful!"

Oh no, not that again…

Monica was on a roll. "I tell you, she's so ungrateful," she fumed. "My dad gave her the chance to be at this school for *free*!"

"Exactly," said her ally. "So ungrateful."

"Then she gets the chance to be in *Mystery* – a movie produced by *my dad*!"

"It's so messed up."

I wanted to stop listening but I couldn't tear myself away.

"Then," Monica continued, "she publicly says I can't act! I tell you, I was born in this industry! Acting is in my blood! I can't believe her nerve. Outsiders have no class!"

That was the knockout blow.

I sat quietly inside the makeup studio while Monty worked on my face. He wasn't making me look ugly this time though, thank goodness. Monty was clearly listening in too. He looked horrified.

I prayed they'd gone, but my prayers fell on deaf ears.

"Mind you, being an outsider is suddenly a good thing. I tell you, if this whole nepotism movement hadn't grown so big, she would never have been offered the role of Saaya, or any other role in *Jigsaw*," continued Monica. "The producers are just trying to prove they're fair to outsiders."

That hurt. That wasn't fair. At least, I hoped it wasn't the case.

"Yeah, that's true, Mon," continued A. "You're a much better actor. Plus you're a model. Bela's only had one rubbish part in a movie. She's just a two-bit dancer."

Monica must have liked that. Because she laughed. Hard. They both did.

By now, I could feel my face flushing red and I desperately wanted them to stop. Of course they knew I could hear them. That was the whole idea.

There was the sound of click-clacking on the floor as they walked off, the cackling finally fading.

"A two-bit dancer?" I tittered nervously when I was sure they had gone. I glanced up at Monty who wore a look of sympathy. "How funny."

I turned my head away from him and focused intently on one spot in the far corner of the room to stop the tears from falling. The last thing I wanted to do was mess up my makeup on the first day of filming.

Monty stepped forward but kept his gaze on my eyelids. "Nearly done!" he announced, blending the green and brown shades on my eyelids until you couldn't tell where one color started and the other ended.

I stared at the rainbow badge Monty wore with such pride. No matter what he was wearing, the badge was always there.

"Close your eyes – let's see properly. Perfect!" He dabbed powder on my face – the final finishing touch. "Okay, *dahling*, I'm done. Now, tell me." He straightened up, folded his arms and took a deep breath. "What on earth was all that about?"

I shrugged. "I don't even know how I ended up on the wrong side of her," I confessed. "It's just so bad…" I remembered Daadi's advice about not getting caught up in any drama.

A little grin appeared on Monty's face. Was he amused by all this? I guess he was used to this kind of thing. But I wasn't. He pulled out a copy of *FilmGlitz* magazine from a drawer.

"Perhaps Monica is reacting to this," he said.

I froze.

On the cover – in big capital letters – screamed the words:

NEPO WARS: OUTSIDERS GANG UP ON STAR KIDS

Underneath was a photo of Monica. *And me.*

I wasn't sure how to react. With horror? Or joy at being featured on the cover of a huge movie magazine?

I had made the cover of *FilmGlitz*! Okay, it wasn't via a glamorous photoshoot, and it wasn't entirely positive coverage, but I was there! Me – the magazine's biggest fan!

I threw an anxious glance at Monty before snatching it out of his hands. The photo showed Monica and me standing with our backs to one another, wearing rather stern expressions. How did they create that image anyway? I'd never posed with her!

"What's this all about?" I asked shakily. "Nothing I've

said has been that bad. She's said much worse things about me!"

I flicked through the pages in a desperate attempt to find the offending article. "Have you read the story, Monty? What does it say?"

"Come on, Bela," urged Monty, taking the magazine back and glancing at the clock. "Don't get yourself worked up. You'll get hot and sweaty and I'll have to do you up all over again."

"But..." I tried to speak but no words came out.

"Look," Monty continued in a calm tone. "Perhaps Monica thinks you're trying to gain advantage by using the Ban Nepotism movement against her. So many star kids are scared these days. They're worried and upset about all the trolling. Monica thinks you're mocking her for being an insider. She's just getting ready to defend herself."

That worried me. The last thing I needed right now was all-out war with the most "in" girl at school. I was desperate to read the full article but I couldn't use my phone until we were on a break.

A harried-looking assistant with a clipboard tapped on the door. She was waiting to lead me back to the set. I quickly followed behind her, passing the dressing rooms and the dance studio, trying to work out how things had gotten this bad. Had I accidentally said something to someone? Was it something I'd written on social media?

By the time I reached the set, my thoughts were weighing me down more than my heavily embroidered dress. Luckily, the senior actors hadn't finished their scene yet so it would be a while before I was called on.

I sat down on an old wooden chair and tried to compose myself. My mind was still whirring – like a wind-up toy you can't switch off – but I was soon drawn into all the action and noise around me. It was so magical to be back on a real set again, and this time I looked the part too.

An emotional scene was being filmed and there was a real sense of melodrama. All the actors, technicians and assistants were fully focused on their duties. Wasted time on set was wasted money, our teachers constantly reminded us. One small hitch could cost the production dearly.

"Hi, Bela," came a voice from behind me. I jumped. I'd been wholly immersed in the scene playing out in front of me. "I didn't recognize you. I thought you were a regular actor – an adult one I mean!" It was Marc. He looked different too. His usual wavy hair had been smoothed down with a side parting.

I looked up at Marc. He towered over me. He looked

so grown up in his traditional Indian outfit complete with a gold, raw silk Nehru jacket. I felt a little shy in his presence.

"Oh," I said, pulling myself out of mute mode. "It's just the makeup." I brushed aside strands of hair that were falling on my face and got up from the chair. As I did, a sudden thought struck me. Had he seen *FilmGlitz* too? Would he also think I was out to get star kids – including him? I felt sick.

"I hear you're leading in the climax dance," he said. "Since you play my love interest!"

I couldn't believe he put it like that! Wait until I told my friends back home – they'd been playfully teasing me about this, especially since they remembered how hooked I'd been on *Rescue*.

"Yeah, I am," I smiled awkwardly. I felt the need to do something so I put on the glittery sandals that the costume department had given me. They only had a one-inch heel but at least that reduced the height difference a little.

I don't know if I was star-struck, having been a fan of his during my childhood, or whether it was because he was an "insider," but I worried he was looking down on me. I always seemed to clam up in his company.

"I heard your aunt is the famous Rita Fernandez?"

I stuttered, saying the first thing that popped into my head.

"Yeah," he nodded. "She is."

"My mom bought me this DVD – *Item Songs by Rita Fernandez* – and we watched it over and over and over. I didn't know she was your aunt until I joined the Academy. I know all the moves from all of her dances," I laughed.

"Yeah?" he commented, dimples on full show. "That's funny."

"My mom's a dance teacher and when I was, like, five or six, she'd be trying to teach me Bharatanatyam and I'd keep dancing to Bollywood songs. Drove her nuts for a while."

"I bet," he smiled. Marc seemed interested in what I was saying, and that made me feel more relaxed.

"So your mom's a dance teacher? That explains your winning performance in Dance Starz," he said. "My aunt was over for dinner that night. We watched it together and she said you were really good."

I gulped. Really? I wanted to jump up and down and scream "YES!" in victory – Rita Fernandez actually watched my performance and she liked it! – but I had to hold it in.

I was wondering what I could say next when I caught

sight of Miss T. She looked at me chatting to Marc and was most definitely trying to communicate something with her eyes – telling us to be quiet, probably. We weren't supposed to be talking "unnecessarily" on set. It was written in what Sophie and I jokingly called the "How To Behave Manual" – basically, the Academy rulebook.

The actors were having a short break. Some were drinking tea while others were surrounded by hair and makeup assistants having further touch-ups.

"Check out Miss T. Could anyone be more moody?" joked Marc, turning his back to her so she couldn't make out what he was saying. "She's always angry because she never made it as a movie star herself." I laughed out loud. I felt bad but he was right.

"I heard about the time she slipped on stage during a play." I spoke in a hushed tone so she wouldn't hear me. "Sophie told me about it."

Marc burst out laughing at the memory and then proceeded to give me the details. He was so animated when he spoke, I felt I could picture it. I joined in the giggling and then we couldn't stop.

Just then, Monica sauntered past us looking eye-catching in a summery white dress with yellow polka dots, bright yellow heels and sunglasses. Even though it was December, the Mumbai winter wasn't vastly different to the summer, just less humid. Monica was with Amrita. I'd guessed right.

As soon as they saw me with Marc, they started whispering to one another. I was sure they were glaring at me.

"Whoa! If looks could kill, Bela!" said Marc, once Monica was safely out of sight.

"Oh no! I bet she thought we were laughing at her," I worried. "I heard her talking about me outside the makeup studio a while ago. I'm pretty sure she hates me. What's she doing here, anyway? I thought she wasn't filming today."

"Well," replied Marc, lowering his voice a little. "She has every right to be here. This is her dad's studio, after all!"

"Showtime Studio as well?" I was shocked. Shashi Kumar was literally Mr. Bollywood, it seemed. A studio in Central Mumbai must have been worth a small fortune. If I wanted to go far as an actor, I really needed to be sure I didn't make an enemy of his daughter. I had to get hold of a copy of *FilmGlitz* to see what it said.

As Marc stood up, Yogi, the director of *Jigsaw*, rushed onto the set and started shouting orders at the unit members to get a move on. I'd met him a few weeks before when he came to the Academy to brief us on the overall timeline and give us our individual rehearsal schedules. He always seemed stressed or deep in thought.

The lighting crew bolted into action, wheeling heavy lighting equipment into its correct positions. The sound technicians put their headphones back on and the beauticians disappeared from view.

"Makeup Monty showed me the cover of *FilmGlitz* today," I blurted out. I had to talk to someone about this – I couldn't wait to get back to my room to discuss it with Sophie. "There's this story in there that says me and Monica are at war."

"Yeah, I saw that," said Marc.

"You did?" I gulped.

"Hmmm. I guess that's why she's mad," he added.

Part of me didn't want to know what it said. The other part won.

"What did it say?" I asked, trying to appear unbothered.

"Oh, I didn't read it all. I try not to get caught up in that stuff," Marc went on, casually leaning back against a pillar. "It's something about you saying that Monica may have the Bollywood breeding, but she's still a B-grade actor. Plus a bit about you saying you've made it on talent and not family connections."

I wanted the ground to swallow me up.

"WHAT?!"

A few people working nearby turned to stare at me. I lowered my voice. "I can't believe it! I have never said that about her."

"Never?" asked Marc.

I recoiled in horror as I remembered the comments both Monica and I had made the day the *Jigsaw* roles had been announced.

"Oh, look," Marc said suddenly, pointing to the film set. "Time to head over. Mr. Yogi's gesturing at us. Don't worry about the magazine, Bela – there's so much fake news out there. Things are twisted all the time."

I nodded. There was nothing I could do about it now anyway. I was determined not to let it affect my performance – this was my time to shine. I smoothed down my dress and followed behind him.

Marc stopped, turned around to look at me, and whispered, "And when you say you love me for the camera, look as though you mean it."

I let out a small nervous laugh. What did he mean by that? But there was no time to think about it. I made a mental note to decipher it once the day was done.

I followed Marc over to where Yogi was waiting. He gave us instructions before positioning us in front of the camera. The lights were pointing directly at us. The noisy chatter around us quickly died down and I suddenly felt nervous even though I had learned my lines religiously over the past two weeks.

Everyone was watching – there must have been at least fifty people staring at me – including Miss T. Thankfully, Monica seemed to have left the studio. Phew.

I breathed and tried to relax. Messing this up was not an option. The last thing I wanted people to think was that I was an undeserving outsider.

The scene we were filming was a flashback scene. In the film, the central character, Vikram, loses his memory after an accident as an adult. He can't remember anything for a long time and then he starts getting flashbacks to his life as a child. So he has to put together the pieces like a jigsaw, hence the name of the film.

In this scene, my character Saaya, Vikram's childhood sweetheart, is at a family wedding and she sneaks away to go and meet Vikram without her family noticing. I needed to look scared and anxious that I might get caught.

I cleared my throat, all too conscious that so many people were staring at me. I had delivered all my lines perfectly the night before, but that was in front of the mirror, in the safety of my room, with just Sophie watching. This was real.

I began: "Vikram, I miss you so much. Papa is trying to stop me from seeing you. I can't do that! I can't live without you. He wants me to change schools but I don't want to leave. I... I... I...love you, Marc."

"CUT!" Yogi yelled. "Bela, Bela, Bela! My darling, whether you love Marc or not is your business, but for the purposes of this film, try to remember you need to call him Vikram."

Everyone on the set roared with laughter.

I wanted to die. I wanted the floor to open up and swallow me. I was crying inside.

"Sorry," I whispered, but the laughter continued.

Marc had tittered too but he quickly realized I was embarrassed. "Okay, come on. It wasn't that funny," he said, scanning the faces of the people around us.

It didn't help much. To make matters worse, when I plucked up the courage to look up again, there was Monica and Amrita standing a few feet behind the camera, laughing their heads off too. In fact, Monica was doubled over, clutching her stomach as though it was so hilarious she couldn't stand up straight.

"I knew it!" she called. "I tell you, Marc, she loves you!"

"Aaah, come on, Monica," he hollered back. "Grow

up."

Monica, none too pleased with that comment, straightened herself up, then linked arms with A and stalked off.

"Don't worry, Bela," said Marc, clearly aware that I was mortified. "It's no big deal. Let's have another go. We've just got to get through this scene. Remember – wasted time is wasted money!"

I allowed myself a smile.

I took a deep breath, recomposed myself and started again. Marc was right. This time there were no mistakes. I delivered the lines with the same emotion as before, then held Marc's hands in mine, gazed into his eyes and with real intensity, whispered, "I love you, Vikram. I love you."

"Cut!" shouted Yogi again. "Wow! That was really good. Very believable. You two have great screen chemistry! You'll be a popular lead pair when you're adults."

I felt proud, but also relieved. It had been a really tough day.

"Top marks, Bela," said Marc. "I knew you'd be fine. You're gonna be one of the very best."

I thanked him and then spent a few moments talking to other crew members. They were all full of praise, including the dialogue writer himself. Miss T looked really pleased, clapping buoyantly, which took me aback. She hardly ever gave praise.

Hoisting my dress up ever so slightly to stop it from dragging along the dusty floor, I began to make my way back toward the dressing room. I was keen to get back to my room as quickly as I could – I was dying to tell Mom about my day. Maybe Jaya was going to call me too? I hadn't gone far though, before I was distracted by the very loud noise of Showtime Studio's main gate scraping over the uneven concrete floor. I turned around to see who it was.

"Shashi Kumar's here," whispered the unit members to one another.

Curious, I watched as a black stretch limousine crawled into the studio forecourt. Shashi indicated to his driver to open the back door of the car and, one by one, a group of schoolchildren emerged wearing dark green and grey uniforms.

"Hello, Shashiji," said Yogi, politely greeting him with a double-handed handshake. "What can we get you? Ramu, go get some water and order tea," he told his assistant.

"Where's Monica?" Shashi asked Yogi. "These children have come from a school where I was attending a fundraising event. They won a talent competition and the first prize is a visit to the studio. I promised them a tour of the set and a meeting with Monica."

As if on cue, Monica walked through an open door at the other end of the studio. In an instant, she was surrounded by the excited schoolchildren as they formed a huge circle around her and demanded her autograph. As she signed flyers and expertly posed for selfies, some people started running towards the studio from the road outside, trying to get into the enclosure. The security guards had forgotten to close the gate and at least a dozen more people had made their way inside.

"Shut the gate!" bellowed Shashi Kumar to the security guards. "What kind of idiot security are you? My daughter's here! I want maximum protection at all times! Full alert, do you hear me?"

At the same time, Monty hurried onto the set with my phone. "You left this on the table," he said, out of breath. "It keeps ringing, and it's driving me nuts!"

"Sorry," I said, taking it from him. I had no idea I had left it and no idea that it was on! I tried to switch it off before Miss T heard it but it went off again.

The children looked around to see where the bhangra ringtone was coming from. Before I knew what was happening, they were all rushing towards me.

"It's Bela! Bela from Dance Starz!" yelled one of the kids. "Bela, please give us your autograph!" they begged, holding their scraps of paper up towards me.

All of the children who had been waiting for Monica were now standing beside me, dancing around, bouncing up and down. Even the few adults who had managed to sneak in were asking me for selfies.

Over by the limousine, Monica was left standing with just a pen in her hand. I hadn't engineered this – it had just happened. But Monica didn't seem to be taking it that way. She narrowed her eyes and flashed the most murderous stare at me before getting into the car and disappearing behind the blacked-out windows.

I signed the autographs, trying to steady my hand. It was as if I might – just might – be on the verge of stardom.

At the same time, I was feeling dread.

I had made an enemy. And a powerful one at that.

TAKE NINE

"No way!" gasped Sophie as we headed down to get Tara for the weekly Movie Night that evening. "Did Monica know you could hear her?"

"Not sure," I replied as we passed the Games Room where students were noisily engaged in an air soccer game. "But she basically listed a whole load of things that I've apparently deliberately said and done to her. What about all the stuff she's said about me?"

"Too bad," said Sophie. "At least Marc was on your side?"

I smiled. "Yeah, he was so sweet. But I still feel stressed out. I hope she won't be at Movie Night tonight. Then again, I shouldn't have to avoid her."

"No, you shouldn't," agreed Sophie. "Don't worry about her. She probably won't be there anyway but even if she is – so what? Stand your ground."

Easier said than done. My feet were reluctant to go any further.

"You know what? Maybe I should give the movie a miss. I didn't even get time to call my parents, and Jaya was meant to call me..." I stopped walking.

"Oh no, you don't!" stated Sophie, holding my arm tightly. "We are going to watch this movie and take your mind off Monica!"

For someone so small and slight, Sophie could be quite forceful when she wanted to be. I gave in with a little nod and we dashed off, taking a shortcut through the pretty courtyard with its incredible Smart Garden, to the wing where Tara's dorm was situated. Her room, on the second floor, overlooked the high-tech garden which featured gigantic flowers with petals created out of solar panels.

I tapped on the door. Tara appeared within seconds, holding up the latest copy of *FilmGlitz*.

"Oh my goodness!" I shrieked. "You got one?"

Apparently Tara had picked up a copy from the library. We ran into her room and pored over the article.

"It's so stupid," I concluded. "It's basically a complete exaggeration. How do they know what I'm saying behind closed doors anyway? Who's telling them?"

"I'm sure there are moles in the Academy," said Tara darkly.

"Well, all the article says is that you think outsiders should be given more opportunities," said Sophie, trying to rationalize it. "Which you kind of said already on Dance Starz."

I nodded.

"*FilmGlitz* has just jumped on this because of all the nepotism stuff going on right now and turned it into a 'war,'" she said, using her fingers for quotation marks.

"I guess so..."

"It's settled then!" decided Tara, grabbing us both happily. "Let's go and enjoy the film. Bollywood, here we come!"

The Observatory was a stunning glass dome attached to the back of the main building. There was fixed, curved seating on one side, and a stage plus pull-down screen on the other. It was always the space used when anybody important or famous came to visit, and students were only allowed to use it for events, like Movie Nights, or special occasions, like graduation ceremonies.

The building was magical during the day when sunlight filled the space and even more so at sunset when the sky was ablaze with different shades of red and pink. It was 8pm now so already dark, and when you looked up, you could see all the millions of stars twinkling in the sky. Watching movies in the Observatory was so cool. It felt like you were sitting in the open air.

Tonight's screening was a "masala movie" – the name given to Bollywood movies that have a mix of everything: songs, action, comedy, melodrama. I always felt moved watching the songs, but it was even more special knowing that I was going to be shooting my first song the following day. Would I even be able to sleep that night?

"That is the kind of movie I want to direct," said Sophie dreamily as the movie ended and the lights came on. "So much action – I loved it!"

"Can we watch another one?" Tara asked Jagdish as he came to clear up at the end of the evening. He just gave her a look. We giggled as we made our way back to our rooms.

I realized it was past 10pm. The Wi-Fi had been switched off, as per Academy rules, so I couldn't even search the internet to see reactions to the *FilmGlitz* piece. Perhaps that was a good thing, I reflected.

I expected Sophie to start getting ready for bed, but instead she gave me a wink and switched on the radio in our room. Music unfurled into the night sky.

Without further thought, we let loose, dancing around the room as if nothing else mattered. It felt wonderful. I really needed it. I could see Sophie looking to me as I danced – she was taking my lead.

Despite all the headaches, stress and nervy moments from the day, I knew that I had made the right decision choosing to come to the Academy. I finally felt that I fit in, that I was known for my dance skills and that people associated me with something I was good at.

I had begun to make my mark at the Academy and hopefully, I would make my mark on the big screen too. That was always going to be my goal.

I was in the right place.

My talent was being honed and, soon, I too would shine like a star.

*

As the bus crawled through the famous gates of Showtime Studio in Central Mumbai once more, I could see that the outdoor set was already a hive of activity. We had been told at our *Jigsaw* briefing by Yogi that the wedding dance sequence would be a real highlight of the movie. The unit members were dashing around frantically, trying to get every detail right for this important scene.

I yawned. I was exhausted. I'd only had time to grab a muffin before leaving the Academy, which I was wolfing down now. I'd stayed up way later than I'd meant to. It had been so much fun dancing with Sophie but I was paying the price now.

As we got off the bus and began walking the short distance to the set, my phone started vibrating. It was a text from Jaya asking me to call her back. She'd have to wait till I was on a break – I had to follow the rules, plus I needed to drink in every detail of what I was witnessing.

The set, made up like a luxurious room in a huge mansion, looked fantastic with its colorful backdrop of gold, red and brown fairy lights. The rich, dark wood furniture with its bright silk upholstery really made me feel as though I was at a wedding. It was a mesmerizing sight.

Miss Takkar ushered us into the Chillout Room where we signed in and were handed the call sheet and our individual itineraries.

Deepa asked Miss T if she could use the "restroom." She had an American accent but insisted she had never been abroad. She'd clearly watched way too many YouTube videos. I thought she looked so cool in her navy Adidas tracksuit with its pink stripes. Her skin was glowing, even without her stage makeup.

Ajay sat down and opened a bottle of Coke Zero. He was on his phone, laughing at something. My heart skipped a beat as I wondered if he was reading about me and Monica.

"Put that away," shouted Miss T, "or it will be taken away!"

Shamim, who was sitting on a floor cushion reading

a cricket magazine, chuckled as Ajay quickly slipped the phone back into his sweatshirt pocket.

I was relieved that Monica wasn't there. I'd heard she was coming straight to the studio from a modeling assignment. I really didn't want any drama so early in the day.

"Bela, you need to go and see Kiran, the choreographer, to rehearse your dance moves," ordered Miss T. "Do you know where the dance studio is?"

I nodded. "I think I passed it yesterday."

"Good, then off you go. But sign out first," she ordered, pointing to the book that acted like a register so that the whereabouts of all the kids could be kept in check by the Academy staff.

I made my way down the corridor, marveling at the framed movie posters that punctuated the walls all the way down. I felt a little giddy at the thought that my face could perhaps grace one of those colorful posters someday. They hadn't got a *Mystery* version up yet, but maybe a *Jigsaw* one would make it?

I pushed open the double doors.

"Hey, Bela," said Kiran, glancing up. She was busily putting out dance mats in preparation for another practice later in the day. "You're bright and early."

I was pleasantly surprised at Kiran's easy manner. She

was such a big name when it came to Bollywood dance that I was a little nervous to meet her. But she didn't seem at all stuck-up. Mom knew the name of every single choreographer in Bollywood. She would be thrilled to hear about this.

"Early maybe, but bright – definitely not," I laughed. "I could have done with sleeping in this morning."

"Yeah, but it'll be worth it when you've done the song," said Kiran, brushing away the dust that had gathered on her black sweatpants. "I watched you on Dance Starz, you know."

"Oh! Nice," I said, flattered that Kiran even knew who I was.

"*One, Two, Three, Naach!* is gonna be one of the big hits of the year, I'm telling you. I knew it the second I heard it. People on the set are already humming the tune."

"I know what you mean," I responded. "I can't get it out of my head either."

"You're a lucky girl fronting this one. It could really help to mark you out as a future leading lady." Kiran smiled. "I've put together some moves for your solo and I want to see if they work for you."

She moved over to the iPhone that was perched on the windowsill. "Let's have a quick run-through."

I took off my sweatshirt and shoes, then dumped

my belongings in one corner of the huge room. Kiran connected her phone to a portable speaker and selected the music. She waited for the first few beats and then came and stood directly in front of me.

I loved the opening notes of the song. I had been listening to it on repeat and it never failed to get me in the mood to dance.

Kiran began by going through the moves for the first verse. Rumor had it, she refused to rehearse songs fully beforehand. She often turned up on a movie set and decided what steps she would use on the very day they were being filmed. Kiran claimed that the music told her what to do.

I watched for ten minutes, awe-struck at how she was improvising as she went along. Then it was my turn. I felt scared but tried to focus. I relaxed my shoulders by forming small circular movements, waited for the music to start, and then began.

As always, as soon as I started to dance, I forgot where I was. There was something about music and dance that made me feel relaxed and happy from within. And it showed on the outside too. I got lost in the moment and felt immediately uplifted.

"Wow, Bela! It's hard to believe that this is the same sleepy-looking girl who tip-toed into the dance studio earlier!"

Trying to move with as much grace and poise as possible, I kept my eyes on my imaginary hero, pretending I was a fully-fledged lead actor.

"That's great!" said Kiran, clapping. "You're a natural, obviously! Okay, let's carry on with me at the front and you behind. Just copy. Ready? 5, 6, 7, 8..."

Kiran played the music from the beginning of the main verse again and I followed, move for move, with almost the same grace. I felt my body flow effortlessly along with the music. I was in the zone. Right there, right then, *that* was what mattered to me. Despite the uncertainties of the profession, I knew it would all be worth it.

"Excellent," commended Kiran once we'd finished the verse. "I can see I don't have to worry about you."

"Thanks!" I was breathless from the multiple twirls at the end but delighted with the vote of confidence.

"Wait here and I'll see if the crew's ready for us. There are loads of extras to deal with today – it's gonna be a long, difficult session."

Just as Kiran was making her way out of the room, Jagdish – who had been appointed as the floor manager of the film – walked in. He was wearing a white half-sleeved shirt with black trousers that were definitely too short for him and he completed the look with black plastic flip-flops.

"Where are you going, Kiran?" he asked with a frown.

"Just checking to see if the extras are here," she replied. "Are we ready to go?"

"Yes, they're all here. Everyone's been briefed," he said. "Which is why I'm here."

Jagdish turned to look at me. I was still standing barefoot in the middle of the room. "We're going to make a slight change to the schedule," he began. "I hope you'll understand."

I felt heat rush up my body, all the way from my toes to my head. My heart raced and my mouth was instantly dry. What did he mean? I could tell it wasn't good news. Jagdish was never this polite.

I looked directly at him but his eyes darted around the room. "The producer, Dev, says it will be better for the film if Marc and Monica are the main focus of the wedding song," he announced, stroking down both sides of his mustache with one hand.

I looked at Kiran in disbelief. This surely couldn't be happening. He must be mistaken! They couldn't just change things like that on the day, could they?

Jagdish took a few steps toward me and then stopped. He looked up at the ceiling and then back down, shuffling his feet anxiously, while I waited for him to provide an explanation.

My chest was tight. There was a lump in my throat and tears were welling up. Gah... Is that why Jaya had been trying to call me?

"But we've rehearsed the song already and Bela's doing a great job," Kiran declared, realizing I needed some help. "I created the steps with her in mind because she's classically trained. Monica's okay, but she moves differently. She's much better suited to modern numbers. Her hips don't move in the same way – it won't work," she finished.

"Look, I'm just the messenger and the decision's been made. That's it," stated Jagdish, ending all possibility of negotiation. "The production house wants Monica to take the lead. No offense, Bela," he concluded, looking in my direction but not directly at me.

"I'd like to speak to Dev, or Jaya, my agent," I said as the tears decided they weren't waiting a second longer. I wiped my face with my hands. "This isn't fair. He can't just change everything around. What about the script? The song's supposed to focus on me and Marc – he's my lead. It won't work if he's dancing with just anyone!"

I was shocked that I had addressed an Academy staff member so directly and wondered if I had landed myself in trouble again.

"He won't be dancing with 'just anyone,'" Jagdish fired back. "He'll be dancing with Monica, and in the movie Monica has a crush on him even though he is dating your character, Saaya. So, you see, it works."

"But–" I didn't get a chance to finish what I was about to say as Jagdish interrupted.

"All this has been thought through. You don't need to worry about it," he continued. "It's for the benefit of the movie, I assure you. Anyhow, Devji is out of town and can't be reached for two days. We have to complete this by tomorrow or we'll fall seriously behind schedule. I have informed Miss Takkar already. We've hired lots of extras for today and they're already here. We're going ahead with it this way, Kiran."

I felt utterly helpless. The fact that he had addressed Kiran at the end and not me made me feel even more insignificant. Maybe I was. I mean, who was I?

I wished I had someone to turn to, but who? I didn't want to bother my family – they would just worry. They were anxious enough about me as it was. They knew all too well that I was fighting an uphill battle most of the time.

I suddenly wondered if this turn of events would affect the fee I received for the film. If it did, that would be an even bigger blow. I could call Jaya, but I wasn't sure what she could do about it.

My brain was whirring, but I was cornered. Jagdish had presented the situation as a done deal and I had no choice but to agree.

"So, Jagdish, you mean to tell me that this has nothing to do with the fact that Dev, the producer, is Shashi Kumar's buddy?" Kiran fired at him. "Is this change really because it's better for the script or just because you're all trying to please Monica's dad? Nepotism at work, hmm?"

"Whatever the reason, it has nothing to do with you," Jagdish retorted, eyes flashing. "And you don't have the right to question it. You're just a choreographer. That's your job, so stick to it. If the producer wants you to make a monkey dance, then that's what you'll do."

He turned his back on Kiran and walked off, his flip-flops slapping against the floor in anger. He tried to slam the swing doors behind him, but they just floated silently closed.

For a few moments, I forgot my own disappointment as my outrage for Kiran took over. She was an incredible talent with countless successful films to her name. She didn't deserve to be insulted for speaking out. I was also humbled by the knowledge that she had been ready to fight for me. It meant a lot.

"That's it? You've agreed to the change?" Kiran turned to me. "I've nothing against Monica, but it's supposed to be the big song of the film and it's unfair to snatch it away from you like that."

I decided I didn't want any more sympathy because then I really would start crying. "Thanks for the support," I mumbled, turning my face away so she wouldn't notice the tears welling up in my eyes. I went to pick up my belongings which were lying in the corner of the room. "If they want Monica, there's not much I can do about it," I added, trying to be as unemotional about it as I could. "But thanks anyway."

I slipped my shoes on, draped my bag and sweatshirt over one shoulder, and walked out of the room.

I truly felt my age. I was just a child thrown into a cruel adult world. No Academy class could have prepared me for this.

I wished my mom was with me. Would the lead song have been snatched away if she had been there?

Perhaps Sonia Soni was right. Maybe Bollywood was best left to insiders.

Once I got back to the set, I joined the other members of the main cast who were standing together watching the production crew set up the shot. There were lots more people around now, some taking photos and videos with their phones. It was very noisy. I made sure I didn't catch anyone's eye. I didn't want to talk about what had just happened.

A few moments later, Marc came and stood beside me. "Ready?" he smiled. I could see he was studying my face. "Is something wrong, Bela?"

I kept my gaze ahead, furrowing my brow and pretending I was concentrating on something. I didn't have any words to explain what had happened and it was too upsetting to talk about it.

Monica was sitting on the bottom step of the false staircase that formed a part of the huge set. She was casually chatting away to one of the makeup assistants. I looked straight at her, hoping she would show some kind of emotion that would indicate whether she had engineered the situation. But Monica's body language gave nothing away.

Jagdish began yelling for everyone to pay attention and get into position. Kiran moved to the front to face the crowd and stood with a loudspeaker. "This is just a run-through," she shouted. "Marc, Monica, to the front. Deepa, Bela, Ajay and Shamim, get behind."

Marc and I took a few steps towards the extras who had gathered on the set. As Marc moved to the front of the crowd, I shifted behind. He looked back at me, confused. Deepa sidled up to me, but I didn't look her way. Instead, I took in the scene in front of me.

Kiran was showing Monica and Marc the very dance moves I had just been practicing.

It hurt so bad.

TAKE TEN

I sat on my bed looking down at my fingernails. A French manicure always looked so nice and natural – I loved the perfect white tips. We weren't usually allowed to wear any kind of nail varnish or makeup while at the Academy, but being a cast member for an actual film meant I had an exemption. Another shooting stint was imminent and preparations were moving full steam ahead.

Six weeks had gone by since I was sacrificed on the altar of Monica in the *Jigsaw* wedding dance number. I had managed to put it to the back of my mind over the Christmas and New Year period, but now that I was back at school and so many students at the Academy had heard about what happened, it was swirling around in my head again.

Since the shoot, only Marc – who had the biggest role – had been needed for filming. But we were now entering the most exciting stint. All eighteen Academy students would be flying to Rajasthan in northern India to shoot for a full five days. The schedule also included a *FilmGlitz* cover shoot for the six actors. I was personally super excited about that. Maybe this was my chance to set the record straight?

"Are you not going to pack?" Sophie asked, jolting me out of my thoughts.

While I was staring at my nails, what I *wasn't* doing was putting all the clothes strewn on my bed into my suitcase.

"You're so lucky," she told me, chewing on a carrot stick. "What I wouldn't do to shoot a movie in Rajasthan!" Sophie sighed dramatically before grabbing another carrot from the bowl.

"Yeah, I guess I *am* lucky," I agreed, getting up off the bed and proceeding to roll all the clothes into tidy sausage-like shapes so that I could cram more into my suitcase. My mom had taught me that trick. It also meant that the clothes didn't crease as easily.

I felt bad that Sophie couldn't join me. "It won't all be fun and games though," I said. "I looked at the schedule yesterday and you know we have to be up at 5am on two of the days?"

"Yikes!" she quipped. "Still, I'd much rather that than stay here."

"Your soccer tournament will be fun too," I said.

"Not quite as much fun as an outdoor movie shoot."

She was right, of course. There was perhaps nothing

better than being part of a big-budget movie, and particularly one shot at the Water Palace in Jaipur!

Daadi would be so proud. We had watched her favorite movie *Mughal-E-Azam* – a period drama – over the Christmas break. Now, here I was, off to an actual, real-life palace that had been inhabited by actual, real-life maharajahs. I couldn't wait. I'd learned about Jal Mahal, the floating palace made from sandstone built at the turn of the 17th century, at elementary school. I'd always dreamed that if I ever became a big star, I'd hold my 18th birthday party there. Imagine that...

"Didn't you say you had to be packed by 3:30?" asked Sophie.

I looked up at the wall clock. Oh no...I'd gotten distracted again. "Argh, help me please Soph – we're leaving in forty-five minutes!"

*

"Oh my giddy aunt! Look at that, it's *flippin'* amazing!" Tara squealed with delight when we arrived at the Water Palace.

Even though she planned on majoring in the Technical Department from ninth grade, I thought Tara would make a far better actor than someone behind the scenes. She was so dramatic and she absolutely loved the limelight.

Tara was right. The Water Palace *was* flippin' amazing. The majestic building was once a hunting lodge and had been enlarged and renovated over the years. It was now a 5-star hotel and rose out of the peaceful, still waters of Man Sagar Lake. It shone white against the striking red night sky. How was it still so pristine, well over two hundred years after it was built? It was a sight to behold.

"First, being bumped up to business class on the plane, and now this... I'm still flying!" exclaimed Tara, squeezing my arm with excitement. Sophie was so calm and laid-back – I needed to recalibrate my brain for Tara. I was also a little floored by the VIP treatment. I could get used to this!

"Line up here. Single file, please," said Mr. Pereira, our vice principal. I couldn't quite work out why he hadn't sent a junior staff member. Did he not have more important things to do back at the school? Somebody had told me he loved a "jolly." It seemed this was true.

We got in line and waited patiently for our ferry to arrive. The only way to reach the palace was by boat as it was literally in the middle of the lake with no bridge to connect it to shore. I felt so relaxed. The air was warm – February in Rajasthan was just perfect – and there was a gentle breeze. A flowery scent hung in the air...or was I imagining it because it completed this picture-perfect scene?

Although some students had groaned and rolled their eyes when they'd heard Miss Takkar would be joining us, I felt the opposite. She could be moody and miserable but there was a kindly auntie feel about her, like she would know if you were really upset. I'd noticed how she had observed me closely when the *Jigsaw* dance scene drama had happened. She was trying to be discreet but she'd kept an eye on me as I'd fought to pull myself together to get through that song sequence and that day.

"Monica, put your phone away," Miss T yelled across us, "or I will take it away. I don't care how upset your millions of followers will be."

Monica tutted and put the mobile in her pocket while A and B whispered to her sympathetically. Marc, Ajay, Shamim and a few other boys ribbed: "How many followers, eh? More than SriLata already?"

"You're all jealous," Monica retorted. "Not my fault I have more followers than all of you combined."

I chuckled. It was true, after all. I couldn't wait to turn thirteen so I could have my own followers but I had to be patient for a few more months.

I watched as the porters fetched the bags from the

private taxis that had ferried us from the airport.
The men looked immaculate. They wore smart, red
velvet tunics with gold buttons that looked somewhere
between military and regal if there is such a thing. They
effortlessly transferred our belongings onto the ferry as
we all filed in.

A few minutes later, we were gliding across the water
towards the palace which became more ethereal and
majestic the closer we came. I took lots of photos so I
could send them to my family when I got to the hotel. I
wished Zara and Daadi could see it for real.

"Wow!" said Shamim. "This is just nuts." He took
some selfies with the palace in the background which his
friends inevitably photo-bombed.

The hotel manager was waiting for us along with two
ladies dressed in orange and white tie-dye sarees. They
held flower garlands and placed one around Miss T's
neck and presented the other to Mr. Pereira.

"Oooh, red carpet treatment!" said Ajay loudly.

Miss T gave him a death-stare before duly informing
us that we would be staying two-to-a-room. Tara grabbed
my arm.

"Miss, Miss, please put me with Bela!"

The guys laughed. She really was a bit extra, but I was
more than happy to be twinning with my friend.

"As long as you promise to teach me some more rhyming slang," I jibed.

"Only if you teach me how to dance like you do," Tara countered.

"Okay, okay let's focus here, please! Everyone get into pairs and I will allocate rooms to you all," announced Miss T.

We all shuffled around a little until we had formed pairs. Well, all of us except Monica. She had two sidekicks and both wanted to share a room with her. A small discussion ensued before it was decided that Monica would, in fact, stay with neither of them. She was told in hushed tones by the hotel manager that an upgrade had been arranged for her and that she could have her own room. Was I even surprised? Bahnaz, being the daughter of a billionaire, could probably have had a whole floor of the hotel to herself but she seemed happy to share with Amrita.

"Bela and Tara, you will be staying in the Rani Room of the palace's residential quarters."

My eyes widened. "The Rani Room? Wow, that sounds amazing."

"All the rooms are amazing here, dear," commented Miss T. "It is, after all, one of the most famous palaces in the world."

"Oh my days," said Tara, mesmerized by the portraits of the maharajahs who had lived and ruled there, lining the corridors that led to our rooms. "There's *nuffink* like this in England, I can tell you."

"Like no Buckingham Palace or Windsor Castle?" I teased.

"Nah, of course we have those. But this is *summink else*."

It really was.

The attention to detail was incredible: the intricate flower patterns carved into the marble walls, the deep, dark pieces of furniture handcrafted from sandalwood, and the ancient metal ornaments on display that dated back hundreds of years.

The head porter, dressed in full Rajasthani finery topped off with a red silk turban, opened the door to our room and neither Tara nor I could quite believe our eyes. It was the most luxurious, sumptuous hotel suite you could ever imagine. It was decorated in rich Rajasthani colors – burnt oranges, pinks and reds – and was so huge, it must have been at least three times the size of our family home.

There was a gorgeous chaise longue on one side of the room and on the other stood two enormous double beds with plump silk cushions. In the far corner by the window was a big desk complete with computer and internet connection. Traditional but with all the mod-cons. Perfect.

Tara dived on to the chaise and kicked her legs in delight. "This is *sooooo* cool! Seriously, it's fit for a queen – Queen Tara of Rajapur," she joked.

I felt like a queen myself – queen of a bygone era. You could almost touch the past. I couldn't wait to share the details of this latest adventure with my besties back home. At times like this, I could hardly believe how lucky I was to be experiencing things I could never even have dared to dream about a year before.

"It's the stuff of ranis, rajahs and maharajahs," I said dreamily.

"You what?" she asked.

"A rani is a queen – come on, you must know that!"

She looked blankly at me. "Well, all I can say," she began, bolting from the chaise and throwing herself onto one of the big, plush beds, "is that you deserve it after all the stuff that's happened with Moni-*cow*. Oops, sorry!" she said sarcastically. "Slip of the tongue."

"Don't! I always seem to land myself in it when it comes to her. The fact that Monica is even here makes me feel uneasy. Like something bad will happen. And I get the sense that *I ain't seen nuffink yet*," I said, mimicking Tara's accent.

"Yeah, we need *Moo*-nica to mind her own business, don't we?" Tara added mischievously.

I laughed. It seemed like there was no stopping Tara when she got going. We chatted about how we expected the next few days would unfold while we unpacked our clothes in our resplendent surroundings.

I was living the dream – for my family, for myself, for outsiders everywhere.

It was the opportunity of a lifetime, and I wasn't going to let anything, or anyone, spoil it.

TAKE ELEVEN

When I stepped onto the set the following afternoon in the stunningly symmetrical courtyard of the Water Palace, I felt all eyes on me – from the Academy students, to the hotel staff, to all the technicians. It was as if I were in some kind of enchanted kingdom and had cast a spell on everyone. I was a little self-conscious but enjoying the attention more than I ever imagined I would.

It didn't escape my notice that Monica was sitting on the colorful sofas with members of the film crew, including the director, Yogi. She was so relaxed around these people, I suppose understandably since she'd grown up in their midst. To me, they were downright scary. I saw her crane her neck to take a look at me, as though to see the final result of my transformation. *Stop focusing on her*, I reminded myself, annoyed that I couldn't shake off her presence.

I was wearing the heaviest, most dazzling outfit you could imagine and a choker neckpiece punctuated with red rubies, both from Mayuri Jain. My whole get-up was so regal, so authentic, like I had stepped out of a history book and come to life. My makeup was flawless – the smudged, smoky kohl made my hazel eyes shine bright – and my hair had been styled into an elaborate bun using hair extensions and secured with dozens of pins. My fingertips, fingernails and toes had been painted red and I was wearing chunky traditional anklets called ghungroos with bells that rang out with each step I took.

Marc, dressed like a prince, was already in position. He was sitting on a throne on a raised platform, and beneath him were the 200 extras – local men who had been drafted in to play the role of foot soldiers. They were dressed in identical outfits: white tunics with red jackets and saffron-colored turbans. Against the white tones of the palace sandstone and the alluring still lake, the scene looked incredible.

My role in this scene was quite straightforward. Vikram dreams that we exist in the late 17th century as Rajasthani royalty but are being separated by our families (us being torn apart was a running theme in the movie). As Saaya, Vikram's sweetheart, I had to scream and protest as I was forcibly led away by members of my ancient, traditional clan, having been caught in a secret rendezvous with Vikram. I had no dialogue to deliver – my facial expressions would be in demand instead. I had learned a lot about this in Mom's Kathak dance classes.

Kathak dance is all about telling a story through dance and facial expressions, so I felt fairly confident that I knew what was required of me. I had already practiced the dance with Sheetal, the choreographer who had taken over from Kiran when she had resigned in protest after the wedding dance debacle.

As they dragged me away, I tried to imagine what Saaya would be feeling. How would she react to being separated from the person she loved? I broke loose from the clutches of my on-screen father – played by a local actor – and launched into my solo dance. It was just two minutes long but I completely lost myself in it. Every fiber of my body was focused. Trance-like, I swayed to the haunting melody, as though lost in a world of pain. My anklets reverberated noisily across the courtyard as my performance hit a crescendo.

I didn't even notice that my dance had put the onlookers into a trance too. When Yogi shouted "Cut!" it was as if someone had clicked a finger and we'd been released from a hypnotic state. There wasn't the usual eruption of cheers. I momentarily wondered if I had made a mistake and that we would need a retake. The cameramen, extras, sound technicians and hotel staff were staring, motionless. The ensuing simple applause, silent acknowledgment and nods of approval, assured me otherwise. I had enchanted my audience and I felt so proud and so glad that Mom had been able to equip me with skills that I had always taken for granted.

I caught another glimpse of Monica watching me, stony-faced. Marc gave me the thumbs-up. Miss T was smiling a proud smile but straightened up when she caught me looking at her, switching back to her usual stern expression.

"Can someone please take a photo of me and Bela?" came a voice I knew all too well. It was the famous dress designer herself. Miss Takkar obliged. I smiled as Mayuri Jain put one arm around me and placed the other on her hip, with her leg strategically positioned at an angle. I had seen this pose so many times by actors on the red carpet – Mayuri was obviously a natural at this.

"I will tag you, Bela dear," she said, taking her phone back from Miss T. I nodded, too embarrassed to tell her that I was too young to have my own accounts yet. I was, however, quite humbled by the interest Mayuri was showing in me. I was also looking at her differently this time around. Mayuri had recently received a lot of flak in the media. She had always boasted about having family links in the industry stretching back decades, but since the nepotism debate had blown up, Mayuri was recounting stories of her struggles as an outsider who had grafted her way up. I was trying to work out which story was true.

She turned to admire me one more time. "It took me six full weeks to make that creation," she said contentedly. "And it fits you like a glove."

She wasn't wrong there.

"And now I can be sure I have the right measurements to start designing your outfit for the movie premiere's catwalk show."

"Sorry?" I spluttered. "What show?"

"*Jigsaw*'s premiere in April. The producers are kicking it off with a catwalk show and live performances," she elaborated.

"Oh, I had no idea."

"You'll be given the details soon, I'm sure. It promises to be something different."

I was curious to know more but Miss T told me I needed to focus on the job at hand. I focused alright. I was exhausted, but satisfied, when the day's filming was done.

It was already evening by the time I slipped out of my costume and into a bathrobe provided by Mayuri Jain – it even had her initials embroidered on the back. The hair and makeup assistants helped reset me back to schoolgirl mode. Makeup wipes removed the heavy foundation and the assistants then carefully removed the pins from my hair, forcing all the extensions to come loose and fall to the floor. They had felt heavy and achy on my scalp all day but I had no cause for complaint. I loved big hair!

I looked at my reflection in the mirror. The uncertainty and trepidation had gone. Was I imagining it or did my eyes now have a look of confidence and assuredness in them?

Back in the Rani Room, I was surprised to see that there was no sign of Tara. Although I was totally exhausted and ready to hit the pillow, I was starving, so I forced myself to shower and change into jeans and a T-shirt before heading off to the restaurant to join the others.

As I approached the dining room, I could hear whooping and loud laughter. *That's strange*, I thought to myself. The dining rooms in the hotel usually had quite a formal atmosphere. A doorman nodded to acknowledge me and opened the door. At first, all I could see was a crowd of Academy students gathered in the middle of the huge room. I walked over to join them, thinking that the palace had put on a comedy act, but I couldn't see what was going on and couldn't hear much because of all the laughter. I managed to squeeze my way past a few people to get closer to the front.

I got the shock of my life when I realized that the comedian in action was none other than Tara. She was standing in the middle of the circle belting out dialogues from old Hindi movies and impersonating popular actors, old and new. Some of the extras and technicians who were staying at the hotel had left their tables to get a closer view of Tara's performance. A couple of the servers had temporarily abandoned their jobs to enjoy the show. They were all in stitches.

I looked around, concerned that one of the teachers might be there and that Tara might get in trouble. I managed to catch her eye. "Tara, what are you–"

"*Oooh*, look who it is," responded Tara in a mock-coy tone. "It's lovely, angelic Bela."

I blushed as all eyes turned toward me and there was a fresh outbreak of laughter. Uh-oh. I could see there was no stopping my friend. She loved attention and there she was, center-stage.

"My name is Bela," began Tara, fluttering her eyelashes. "You must all know that I'm just *soooooo* sweet. I've worked my way up to the top, unlike...ahem...*Moo-nica*..."

I gasped and looked around to see if anybody understood what she was talking about. Tara carried on.

"Monica's okay...for a nepo-kid. But would she actually get any jobs without her parents' help?"

The onlookers were really laughing now and some of the students were recording Tara's act on their phones. I didn't know whether to laugh or cry. I was glad that Monica didn't appear to be in the room.

"And now, ladies and gentlemen, for my final performance," announced Tara with much aplomb. I looked on, dreading to think what might be coming next. Tara put on a sultry pout and struck a model pose, flicking her hair away from her face with attitude.

"I tell you, I need no introduction because everyone knows me. I have seventy million social media followers after all..."

Ajay and Marc were in fits. Shamim was hooting and clapping. "Right on the mark," he shouted. Tara smiled and then continued striking model poses. "My dad is the famous Shashi Kumar and, I tell you, as you all know, he, like, owns Bollywood. My mom was a star too. I tell you, Bollywood is in my blood. In fact, my blood sings and dances as it travels through my veins..."

I raised my hand to my mouth, trying to stifle a giggle. It was a stupid sketch, but Tara's voice, movements and style mimicked Monica so perfectly that you couldn't help but be amused. Tara continued pouting and the audience carried on applauding until finally, I couldn't hold back. I was full of confidence after the day's shoot and for the first time I was beginning to feel that I was being accepted. I allowed myself to join in. I laughed really hard.

It was only when Mr. Pereira got wind of what was going on and rushed into the dining room that Tara ended the impromptu show by darting into the crowd and hiding behind me. The servers hurried back inside the kitchen, the diners strolled back to their tables, and Tara and I rushed to the back of the line for the buffet.

"You are terrible, Tara. Just...terrible!" I said, feeling self-conscious and trying not to catch anyone's eye. I was still recovering from my fit of giggles but working on calming myself down so that I could tell Tara she was playing with fire.

"What if Monica had come into the dining hall?" I asked.

"What if she had?" Tara countered. "It's the least she deserves."

"But, Tara, I've had so much trouble with her already. The last thing I need is an actual reason for her to hate me."

Tara turned to look at me before scooping freshly cooked rice made with cumin seeds onto her plate.

"She doesn't hate you because of anything you've said to her," she told me. "Or anything you've done. It's because she's jealous of you, innit?"

I scoffed. "No way is she jealous of me – I mean, why?"

"I saw her today. When you were giving that performance of a lifetime, you should have seen her face. She was looking around at everyone and hated that they loved how you danced. And she probably hated that you looked drop-dead gorgeous too."

I listened.

"Don't you see? She's threatened by your talent. Threatened by the fact that you're here *because* of your talent. She sees you as her biggest rival."

It finally dawned on me. Tara was right. I'd never imagined Monica would be threatened by me. Maybe "the look" Monica had given me in the Dance Starz final hadn't been down to any comment I'd made on stage. It could have been for the simple fact that she saw me as competition.

I was on a high, riding the crest of a wave. I no longer felt that I wasn't good enough or that I was somehow inferior to a star kid like Monica.

I had talent. I had skill.

I finally felt like I had earned my place at the Bollywood Academy.

*

"I've been hearing all about Tara's little performance last night," Miss Takker said to me as I stood in the breakfast line. I had been admiring the scrumptious options – every type of melon, mango and exotic fruit you could think of, plus delicious pains au chocolat and hot buttery toast. "I'd never have guessed she was an impressionist. Where is she?"

I quickly averted my gaze. The view was to-die-for – the lake looked so peaceful and serene as the sun rose and cast a stunning reflection over it – but maybe this wasn't the best moment to be admiring it.

"She's showering, Miss," I said, holding up my plate so the chef could dish up an omelet. "She'll be down in a minute."

"I didn't see the live rendition, but Tara seems to be the talk of the palace," she went on. "In fact, someone's even gone to the bother of putting her sketches up on YouTube."

"Huh?" I responded, trying to play it down but secretly wanting to drop my plate and scoot all the way to the Rani Room to watch it with Tara. "YouTube? Oh my goodness, how did that happ–"

As soon as the words left my mouth, I remembered

some of the kids filming Tara on their cell phones.

"If you type in 'Water Palace' it comes straight up," said Marc as he passed by with his plate of food.

"Well, she'll need to have words with Mrs. Arora when she gets back to school," Miss Takker informed me. "We're on a tight schedule here – the focus has to be on getting today's shooting done. But rest assured that as soon as we get back, we'll be having words."

"Yes, Miss," I muttered. I grabbed a glass of freshly-squeezed orange juice, placed it on my tray and found myself an empty table that wouldn't be in Miss T's line of sight. As soon as I was sure she wasn't watching me, I messaged Tara.

"Get yourself down here NOW!"

Right on cue, Tara walked in. I motioned for her to come over. "Whassup?" she asked.

"Apparently, someone has put your late-night impersonations on YouTube. Miss T was telling me..."

"No way!" she said, cupping a hand over her mouth. "*No way!*"

She sat down next to me while I hurriedly keyed "Water Palace" into Google. My eyes widened as I noticed that the first video that came up – with 98,000 views! – was *the* video.

"Looks as though you're famous, Tara!"

Tara squeezed my arm as I played the clip of her impersonating me. Within seconds, we were both laughing again.

"I am not at all like that, Tara Sharma!" I said.

"Let's see if there are any more," said Tara keenly.

"Go get your breakfast," I urged her. I noticed that some of the students on the other tables were looking over at us. "And I should warn you – Miss T said you'll have to see Mrs. Arora once we get back to school."

"Oh, is that so?" she fumed. "There's no law against performing, is there? All comedy acts include impersonations."

"Yes, but you're not a comedy act, Tara," I said, scrolling down the list.

My eyes stopped at one particular video. "What's this?"

Tara began to read: "Bela laughs at Monica."

"Oh no," I said, trembling a little. I clicked hesitantly on the link.

The recording began with a brief shot of Tara pouting and posing as Monica. The camera then panned in on my face alone, showing me clapping and laughing uncontrollably. When you looked at it that way, a close-up of my face and nobody else in focus, it seemed as though I was the only one encouraging Tara's mockery of

Monica.

My heart sank. Was this going to turn into another ill-fated incident with Monica? The timing couldn't have been worse.

At that instant, Monica sauntered into the dining room with her friends. I thought I might have seen Amrita in the crowd during Tara's performance. Had she posted the video?

The trio walked toward the breakfast bar to collect their food and, as they passed by our table, Monica stopped. She turned to look at me, then Tara, then me again. And she held her stare for what seemed like minutes. She didn't say a word but her expression said it all. I held my breath until she moved off.

I looked at Tara. Tara looked at me. We both knew it.

Somehow, I had landed myself in it again.

Somehow, the joke was on me.

TAKE TWELVE

I aimed to keep a low profile for the last two days of the shoot. And, of course, to keep out of Monica's way. I still wasn't sure how angry she was with me or Tara. Somehow, her silence was the most terrifying part.

I was glad I wasn't filming any scenes that day, though I still had to go along and spend the whole day on set since we weren't allowed to stay in the hotel unaccompanied. I sat quietly in one corner of the porch for most of the day. The open area with its glass roof and patterned marble floor was positioned perfectly – within viewing distance of the courtyard that formed our set but far enough away for me to remain unnoticed. I hung out with Tara, of course, when she wasn't darting about. She had to do a lot of running around with equipment and props for the sound and lighting departments.

"Looks like you haven't got much to do down there," I joked when she came up for a break.

"You're having a bubble, aren't you?" she replied.

"Huh?"

"Bubble bath. Laugh, obvs!"

"Oh! Of course," I grinned.

"They're killing me," she said, wiping sweat from her brow with her T-shirt sleeve. "I thought I'd be standing around, casually watching the scenes unfold. It's child labor, I tell you!"

"Well at least you only have a couple of days left," I said.

"You know, I bumped into Monica while I was helping the lighting guys?"

"Oh?" I squeaked.

"I thought she might say something – or yell at me even. Monica is strangely non-bothered by the vids, don't you think?" Tara questioned, offering me some Cadbury's chocolate her mom had sent over from England. She swore it tasted nothing like the Indian version.

"Hmmm," I replied. I'd been wondering the same thing. Did her silence mean she was plotting revenge? I shuddered at the thought but couldn't come up with a better explanation.

"Perhaps she realizes it's not such a big deal," said Tara.

"Are you kidding me? It's all over social media!" In fact, some of the desperate Bollywood news feeds had even created stories out of Tara's video. They would post literally anything that would get likes or clicks. Even stupid stories showing the "airport style" of some of the leading actors. I mean, what even is that?

The videos of Tara's performance were circulating and they were hardly flattering, but perhaps Monica was too involved in filming to care?

I could see her clearly from where I was sitting. She was dressed in an outfit that was almost as remarkable as mine had been. It had hues of bottle green and royal blue. The rich combination of colors really set off her hair. With her skin so pale and her hair so dark, the dress made her look like a peacock, if it's at all possible for a girl to resemble one. And as much as it pained me to admit it, she moved with the grace of one too.

Each time she caught me looking at her, I pretended to be talking to somebody or reading my book. We actually had some big exams coming up a couple of weeks after we got back and I was determined not to leave all the studying to the last minute. At stage school, you never knew when an opportunity might come up that would demand your time so I was always trying to keep on top of my work.

No sooner had I had the thought than a message pinged on my cell phone.

Sorry Bela, my cell is acting up so using this number until fixed. I can't recall your mom's number so am messaging you

*cos it's urgent. I had a call from a Netflix agent interested
in casting you for a high school series. There will be 6 eps in
season 1. Shooting begins in June for a 3-month stint. Directed
by Om Shankara! He is close by in Rajasthan finishing a
movie and can meet you tomorrow. Let me know if interested
and I can send you the address. Jaya. X*

"Wait. What!?"

I was trying to make sense of what I had just read.
Netflix?! I scanned it again, my eyes struggling to take in
the words in front of me.

"Breathe," I told myself.

I looked up and saw Monica dashing from her trailer
to the set with a different pair of shoes. She slipped her
feet into them and got back to her position alongside the
other girls in the shot. Tara had seen the head of lighting
motioning to her so had rushed back down again.

I still hadn't actually met Jaya in person. She always
had excuses for why she couldn't come – she was busy
with this, that or the other. Mom wasn't happy. She felt
Jaya was doing zero work to get me contracts but was
taking a 15% cut for work I was getting under my own
steam. Maybe she was finally coming through for me?

I hurriedly typed out a text to Mom.

*Mom! OMG guess what? Jaya said Netflix wants to cast
me in a series! Directed by Om Shankara – your favorite! I*

have to make a decision today as he wants to meet me here in Rajasthan tomorrow. I'm gonna say yes and then Jaya will send address!

I was bursting with excitement. Om Shankara was the biggest film director in India, and Netflix the biggest streaming platform. I couldn't have asked for a more high-profile opportunity than this! Being away from my family was a sacrifice, but it would be worth it if I landed this part. My parents wouldn't have to struggle so much. Maybe I could help support them so they could have all the things they dreamed of? And, above all, I would be giving hope to millions of other outsiders like me. I'd be showing them that it was possible to break down barriers and succeed. Maybe I could pave the way for Zara to have a career in the industry too? My little sis would be so proud!

I couldn't wait for the day's filming to be over. It seemed to take forever, but as soon as we were back in our room, I let loose.

"Guess what!" I screamed, grabbing Tara's arms and pulling her into a tight hug as soon as she walked in.

"Whoa, girl! What's going on?"

"Guess what? I might get chosen for a Netflix series and it's going to be directed by Om Shankara!" The words just tumbled out.

"Haha," she laughed, clapping her hands at what she thought was a joke.

"It's not a joke!"

"Wait, what? Really?" she asked, blinking animatedly. "Like, *really*?"

"Really!" I shrieked.

"Would you Adam and Eve it?" she yelled.

"You mean 'believe it?'" I was getting the hang of this now.

"Yes! Would you believe it? Bela in an Om Shankara series!" With that, Tara grabbed my hands and we jumped up and down. She then proceeded to sing and dance around the room. She had so much energy – I got tired just watching her. It was heart-warming to see how thrilled she was for me.

One thing I'd realized was that in this industry, there was a lot of jealousy. People were more likely to tear each other down than prop each other up. I was lucky to have good friends who had my back, both at the Academy and at home.

"Don't forget me when you're rich and famous," beamed Tara, planting herself down on the bed. "Do you think the YouTube vid helped? Is that what made you clinch it?"

"Maybe," I pondered. "Mom always says there's no

such thing as bad publicity..."

We chuckled. It was strange – the rollercoaster highs and lows of this world meant that a big event from yesterday could feel like it happened so long ago simply because the next event was even bigger.

My phone beeped. It was a message from Mom.

Mom: *Okay strange that Jaya didn't text me first. She usually does.*

Me: *Her phone isn't working Mom. She couldn't remember your number.*

Mom: *Okay no problem. I will email her tomorrow after your meeting. Who will go with you?*

Me: *Miss T or Mr. P I guess. I'll let you know.*

Mom: *So happy for you. Daadi hasn't stopped dancing! Zara is so excited too. Good luck for tomorrow!*

"When is the audition?" Tara asked when I looked up.

"Oh, that reminds me – I have to text Jaya and ask for the details. Maybe the meeting is like an informal audition?"

The thought that I might be asked to do an impromptu audition or dialogue recital was niggling at me. I grabbed my phone and typed a message to Jaya.

Five minutes later, she replied.

Mansingh Palace, Vaishali Nagar, Ajmer – 305001. Meet in the reception area at 11am.

"Ajmer? Where's that?" I clicked on my Maps app. "Two hours 39 minutes! And I need to be there by 11am?"

"Don't worry about that," Tara reassured me. "Miss T will go with you, won't she? It's a big one for the Academy if you get it."

We both looked at each other.

"A missed audition is a missed opportunity," we chimed, smiling.

A sudden realization hit me like a ton of bricks.

"It's not who'll take me that's worrying me," I said, my smile fading. "Tomorrow is the *FilmGlitz* publicity shoot!"

"Oh?" said Tara.

"It's the big cover shoot to tie in with the release of *Jigsaw*. All the Academy cast – the six of us – are meant to do it. It's on my filming schedule." I waved the piece of paper that Miss T had given to me at Tara.

"I have to sort this out with Miss T. See you in a minute," I said, reaching for my shoes and running to the door.

I dashed down the corridor and then stopped. I wasn't even sure where Miss T was. I ran down to reception.

"Please can you call Miss Takkar's room?" I urged the receptionist.

"Miss Takkar is in the bar." She pointed to a door.

I speed-walked over to the room and entered. She was having a drink with Mr. Pereira and didn't seem too happy to see me.

"Sorry, Miss," I said. "It's urgent."

"Yes?"

"Miss, I have a big job coming up. It's an Om Shankara project and I have to meet him tomorrow otherwise I might not get it and tomorrow is the day of the *FilmGlitz* cover shoot and I'm supposed to be on the cover so I don't know what to do and who can take me."

"Take a breath, take a breath, Bela!" said Mr. Pereira. "You said Om Shankara?"

"Yes, sir."

"*The* Om Shankara? As in the biggest director in Bollywood?"

"Yes, sir."

I showed them the text messages and it seemed they were both working things out in their heads.

"Well, you wouldn't want to pass up an opportunity like this. You need to go," decided Mr. Pereira. "I will take you since Miss Takkar will be busy with the cover shoot."

Miss Takkar looked surprised. "Mr. Pereira, it's quite alright. *FilmGlitz* will be sending a hair and makeup team. Plus two photographers. So I really won't be needed here."

"I insist," he said firmly. He clearly had no intention of letting anybody else enjoy the biggest perk of his job. Miss Takkar looked at him and pursed her lips.

I was so amused by this. They both wanted to go on a six-hour round trip? Were they both super-fans of the director?

"It's decided then. I will take you to Ajmer. I'll pop over to reception now to arrange a taxi for the day."

"Do I miss the shoot then?" I asked.

Miss T's eyes burned a hole in me. She seemed to be annoyed with Mr Pereira's decision. "You know that you can't be in two places at once, don't you, Bela?" she snapped.

I nodded.

"Go on, then. What's it going to be?"

It was agonizing. Like choosing which of your friends you liked more. I so wanted to shoot for *FilmGlitz*, especially since the first (and last) time I had been featured, it was that terrible mocked-up image about a war with Monica. That had been horrible. This was my chance to fix it. But...

I took a deep breath in.

"Om Shankara meeting," I decided.

I hoped I had made the right choice.

Of course I had.

If I landed the Netflix role, there would be many more cover shoots lined up for me.

I would no longer have to prove myself or struggle for small jobs against the girls who were guaranteed to get roles due to their connections.

It was a no-brainer.

TAKE THIRTEEN

I was still on cloud nine when I went downstairs the next morning. I felt like the cat that caught the canary.

Overnight, I had followed Om Shankara on all of his socials and had even commented on his recent posts. I didn't want to give it away yet so just wrote: *Love your work, sir. I look forward to working with you some day!*

I had then gone on to share the news with Priyanka, Ayesha and Reshma on a group chat with a big "PROMISE YOU WON'T TELL ANYONE!" There was no way I was going to share this news with anybody except for my inner circle. I couldn't trust it not to get out.

I sat with Tara in the Tea Garden. It was so quaint with its round, cast-iron tables that had been painted in pastel shades. The waiters circulated with trays of juices, teas, coffees and sweet-smelling masala chai. Ajay came over to our table. I had hardly ever spoken to him although I was seeing him around a lot these days, either with Marc or on set as a co-star.

"Hey, Bela."

"Hi," I said, taking a bite of my croissant and

conscious that the little pastry flakes were stuck to my face.

"Guess what I heard?"

"What?" I asked.

Marc was sitting with Shamim and a couple of the technicians at the very end of the garden under the shade of a tree. He waved at us.

"O.M..."

I stared blankly at him.

"Om..." he said.

My heart skipped a beat. Did he know?

"Oh, that," I said casually.

How did he find out? Did the others know? What would Monica make of it? Was she jealous? Questions raced through my mind at the speed of light.

"So, it's true? You got a role in Om Shankara's first TV series ever? You know how big that will be?!"

"Well, it's in the pipeline. I'm off to meet him now," I replied, as though this sort of thing happened every day.

Monica and her friends glanced over and then looked away. They huddled together over their cups of tea as if they were discussing something secret.

"Come on, Bela," said Mr. Pereira. He smoothed down his sunshine yellow tie. "The driver is waiting."

We made our way to the taxi.

Mr. Pereira was much chattier than usual on the journey. He seemed more like a normal person than the Vice Principal and we talked a lot about movies and TV shows. Mr. Pereira admitted he really admired Om Shankara's work although he was careful not to come across as a fanboy. The driver didn't care to join in. He was listening to folk songs on the radio.

I looked out at the Rajasthani scenery as we drove. I wondered if I'd get to see any of the state's famous desert. This just looked like dry, barren land. The area could really do with some rain, it seemed. I decided I preferred the humidity of Mumbai.

It was 10:50am when we pulled into the long sweeping driveway leading to the Mansingh Palace. It was a magnificent hotel. There was nothing dry about this place – the plants and trees were lush and green. I'd read that the building was a replica of a fortress. Perhaps it wasn't quite as grand as "our palace" but it was number two on my all-time favorite list for sure.

The driver parked up under the shade of a big tree and we made our way in. I was nervous and asked Mr. Pereira if I could use the restroom. It was the kind of restroom you wanted to stay in forever but I didn't have time to revel in its charm. I applied some clear lip gloss to add a touch of sparkle to my look – maybe Miss T would have suggested light makeup? I adjusted the straps on my dress, wondering whether I should drape a cardigan casually over my shoulders.

I made my way towards the reception desk, thinking Mom must be in the mandir right now donating food in return for good luck so I could get the part.

Mr. Pereira was speaking in a slightly raised tone.

"No, I'm sure you've got this wrong. Can you please ask the hotel manager? Om Shankara is a big director. I am certain he doesn't advertise his whereabouts."

I stood next to Mr. Pereira as the reception guy went off to fetch the manager.

"The silly fellow said that Om Shankara isn't here and isn't due here. Can I check the address on your phone again?"

I passed it over to him.

"Yes – see! It's the same place, same postal address."

The hotel manager came out and invited us to sit down.

Mr. Pereira explained.

"I'm sorry, sir, but nobody is aware of Mr. Shankara staying here. If he is visiting for a meeting, then I would suggest you wait."

So we sat down and waited. I was tapping my foot repeatedly on the floor but stopped when I realized Mr.

Pereira was watching me. He took out a handkerchief and dabbed his forehead. The receptionist brought over two glasses of orange juice and a jug of water – with compliments. The staff could see that Mr. Pereira was anxious and didn't want a scene in their lobby.

Half an hour passed.

Then an hour.

Nothing.

We called Jaya but it went to voicemail.

I grabbed a glass of water and took a few gulps. Mr. Pereira, who had seemed so relaxed and laidback on the way down, was now irritated and angry.

As for me, I wondered if I would be sick. My dream was turning into the worst possible nightmare. Did Om Shankara forget? Did the series just get canceled? Did Jaya get the wrong end of the stick? What if we had to turn around again?

I couldn't even begin to fathom whether the embarrassment of coming all this way for nothing would be worse than missing out on the *FilmGlitz* photoshoot.

Okay, calm down, I told myself. *Breathe*. There had to be an explanation. Om Shankara might be late – famous people were always late! He might have gone to the wrong hotel? Totally plausible.

"Let me try Jaya's old number, sir," I suggested,

praying I would get through.

The phone rang. I smiled. "Phew." Jaya would get to the bottom of this.

"Hello?" said Jaya. I had never been so glad to hear her voice. The words tumbled out of my mouth so fast, I hoped I was making sense.

"What are you talking about, Bela?" said Jaya sternly after she had heard me out.

"You texted me yesterday evening from the other number."

"What other number? I don't have another number."

My mind went blank.

I had read the messages so many times, they were ingrained in my memory. I repeated what they said.

"Hand the phone to Mr. Pereira," she said with a note of urgency in her voice.

He took the phone and said very little. He nodded and then looked over at me. He nodded some more. He passed it back to me.

I knew what was coming. I had worked it out.

There was no audition.

There was no Om Shankara meeting.

There was no Netflix series lined up for me.

Somebody was pulling a prank.

I put my head in my hands and sobbed my heart out.

*

The journey back was so painful. We barely spoke. Mr. Pereira had been fairly sympathetic when I had broken down in the hotel lobby but I don't think he knew quite what to say. I switched my phone on during the drive and then, seeing all the messages from people congratulating me on the Om Shankara series, switched it off again.

When we reached the Water Palace later that afternoon, Miss Takkar was waiting for us at the entrance. Mr. Pereira had obviously texted ahead to tell her the disastrous news.

Miss T welcomed me with a warm smile and gave me a hug, which made me feel even worse. For Miss Takkar to be so affectionate, it meant that the situation was really bad. Tears rolled down my face and I stepped back, mortified at the turn of events.

"Come with me, Bela. They're just finishing the cover shoot," Miss T said enthusiastically. *She's not reading the room right on this one*, I thought. How was that going to make me feel better? I just wanted to curl up in a ball and hide in my room.

I reluctantly followed Miss T into the hotel. I had wasted the Academy's time and money on this horrendous trip so I felt like I had to grit my teeth and bear it.

The photographer was kneeling on the floor of the marble terrace photographing Marc, who wore traditional Rajasthani clothes made from off-white silk, embellished with gold thread. A rustic silk turban completed the look. Monica, Deepa, Shamim and Ajay were also dressed in traditional attire. Monica was positioned at the center of the group, alongside Marc.

"One last shot," shouted the photographer to his assistant. "Go grab those two thrones."

Monica and Marc sat down on the red velvet chairs with gold arm rests and the others stood behind them.

"This'll make a great cover," enthused the snapper. "Headline: The Future King and Queen of Bollywood."

The words "salt" and "wound" came to mind.

"That's a wrap!" shouted the photographer a few minutes later. The group whooped with joy and high-fived each other.

"That was so much fun!" clapped Monica. She looked mesmerizing in an organza crop top and skirt outfit, which made it all the more sickening if that were possible.

"We're done!" said Miss Takkar, trying to energize me. "You played such a big role in the film too! Come, let's go down and celebrate."

I dragged my feet towards the group.

They saw me approaching.

Marc gave me a commiserating smile.

"You look nice, Marc," I mumbled.

"Thanks. We missed you today. Sorry to hear about what happened," he said. I could feel everyone's eyes on me. From the *FilmGlitz* crew to the Academy students to the hotel staff.

Everyone knew? Already?

Of course they did...

"I wonder who could have been behind the cruel hoax?" questioned Monica as she linked arms with her friends.

Yeah, sure you think it's cruel, I thought to myself. I had zero evidence, but nobody disliked me as much as Monica. She was my number one suspect. I thought back to the way she'd been giggling with her friends that morning at breakfast... Very suspicious.

Miss T was suddenly very serious.

"We will get to the bottom of this matter, Bela. We'll report it to the relevant authorities who will investigate."

"We're as shocked as you are, Miss," said Amrita who'd been eagerly taking behind-the-scenes footage of the shoot on her phone. "We all believed it when we heard Bela had been offered a Netflix series."

"I tell you, if it hadn't been so hush-hush, like it was classified information, and we'd all been told, I would have worked it out," interjected Monica. "I mean – what top director would invite just one eighth grade student to audition for a top Netflix show at a day's notice? Who wouldn't hear those alarm bells?"

She had a way with words.

Put like that, I felt so small.

But not small enough.

I wished I were invisible.

*

I lay in my bed. Very still.

I could hear the birds chirping outside the window. I imagined they were kind friends trying to make me feel better, offering words of sympathy. But nothing felt like consolation.

The humiliation was real and complete.

The way I'd fallen into the trap – which now, of course, seemed so obvious – was devastating. I was a laughing stock.

And to think that I'd believed it was real. What was I thinking when I'd commented on Om Shankara's posts? What must he have been thinking if he had seen my comments? Or worse still, found out exactly how stupid and naïve I was?

Tara was fast asleep – snoring away in the gigantic bed next to me.

We were leaving Rajasthan to go back to the Academy that day. This luxurious suite had lost all its gloss and charm. I didn't care for the hotel's five-star service and grandeur. I just wanted to go home. I felt so low, I wondered if I would even be able to muster the strength just to pack and be ready for the flight back.

Jaya's messages had hurt. Words like "inconceivable" and "irresponsible" seemed like they had been typed in bold font and underlined.

Mom's apologies – for falling for it and encouraging me to go – were designed to make me feel better but they didn't.

My brother Reuben had been less sympathetic. *How did you think you would land such a big role like that – with an impromptu meeting out in Rajasthan? Arranged through an anonymous number?* he had chided via text. He must have felt a bit bad though because he messaged me later to ask if I was okay.

Ajay and Marc had been kind.

"Don't worry," Marc had said with a sympathetic smile. "In the big scheme of things, it's nothing really.

Nobody died. You lost nothing."

True, nobody had died.

But I had lost something.

Confidence. Dignity.

And above all, the belief that everything would be okay.

TAKE FOURTEEN

"Oh, Bela, I missed you!"

Sophie grabbed me the second I'd wheeled my suitcase into the room and closed the door behind me.

It was just what I needed. A kind, familiar face – a hug from someone who was on my side.

"I missed you too," I said. I meant it.

Tara must have told her about the hoax since Sophie had texted saying: *It wasn't your fault Bela. You could never have known you were being set up!*

"What's with the shades?" Sophie asked. "It's dark outside!"

I removed them, and the baseball cap. They'd helped me feel more anonymous on the long journey home.

I hadn't wanted to talk to anyone on the trip back. It'd been hard enough dealing with the shame of falling into a trap. On top of that, I was mourning the loss of a television series that had never existed in the first place. And a fee that could have helped my parents. And to think that I had started to feel like I was being accepted... Now I felt like I was out in the cold again, looking in.

"Are you going down to eat?" Sophie asked, looking

concerned. She was already in her PJs. "I've just been, but I'll go with you if you want me to?"

"It's okay, Soph. I'm not hungry. And I'm fine."

"Are you sure, Bela?" she said, raising an eyebrow. "I can't believe..." Sophie faltered. "I just don't get why someone would do that. The school will investigate, won't it? I can't believe the teachers fell for it too! And who was it?"

I shrugged my shoulders. "Doesn't matter who. And I don't know if the school can do anything. The text was sent from an unknown number."

I had gone through the whole incident in my mind over and over again on the trip home. It hadn't helped at all and I was well aware that I had to get over it. Exams were coming up.

"Dad is so upset, he told me to come home," I said.

"For a holiday?"

"For good."

Sophie's mouth opened wide. Then closed. It was clear she didn't know what to say.

"Why?" she asked eventually. "Just because of this?"

"Mom sees it as bullying. I didn't do anything wrong but I've been made to look like a fool. And I missed out on the *FilmGlitz* shoot," I said, tears threatening again. "Dad is so mad right now. He thinks I should forget about movies and stuff until I'm older. Maybe he's got a point."

"But you're so good, Bela! You can't give up now." Sophie came and sat next to me and put an arm around my shoulder.

I sighed. "I've always wanted to dance – to be a Bollywood actor or stage performer – but I'd never planned for it to happen so young," I explained. "Mom was the one pushing me to enter Dance Starz. She's always said that you never know when you'll get another chance. She didn't want me to have regrets later on." I wiped away a tear. "It all started because I really wanted a phone." I shook my head while Sophie looked on sympathetically.

My path to the Academy had been one crazy ride. My simple uncomplicated existence in Chandivali's Sector R2 seemed like a lifetime ago.

Sophie reached out and hugged me tight. She was definitely also #friendslikefamily. It didn't take away the pain but it did give me a little strength to carry on.

She had already given up on her dreams to be an actor.

I wasn't certain I was ready to give up on mine just yet.

*

Over the next few days, I felt numb – as though I was on auto-pilot. I went to classes and then straight back to my room, to bed. Everything seemed like hard work. I felt distracted and detached. I tried hard to revise for finals which were just a couple of weeks away but found it so tough.

Dad kept asking me about revision, exams, test grades. Mom kept asking me about the movie as though she was worried my role would be cut again. I kept telling her that *Jigsaw* was in editing – I had zero control over it earlier and even less now, if that were possible.

I tried to stay upbeat when I spoke to Daadi and Zara. I didn't want them to worry. But constantly trying to please everyone was hard, especially when I felt so unmotivated and deflated myself.

I'd been on the verge of speed-dialing Priyanka a couple of times but then stopped myself. Would she understand? She would probably think I was being ungrateful. Even though I'd filled Priyanka, Ayesha and Reshma in on some of the "beef" with Monica, I'd spent more time sharing details of the sparklier aspects of my stage school. They'd wanted to see photos of film sets and selfies of me with perfect makeup courtesy of Monty, so that's what I'd served up.

Maybe if I had been more honest with my friends, I wouldn't feel so burdened now. Like I was sinking.

"How are you managing to do all this revision?" I asked Sophie as I lay down with my comforter pulled up to my chin.

"Huh?" Her nose was stuck in a textbook. "You should revise too, Bela. You can't wing it in Biology or Math. Just do an hour a day."

I turned over and pulled the comforter up even higher. I couldn't bear the thought.

I closed my eyes and went to sleep.

*

I should have seen it coming, really. I didn't deserve to pass. But I didn't deserve 26% either. I was a 70%+ student! So how come my mind felt like mush?

And why was I feeling so low?

I was spending more and more time in my dorm now. I'd always enjoyed swinging by the library and the TV room, or for walks around the grounds after school hours, but I didn't want to see anyone now – especially not *you-know-who*.

Mr. Pereira had told me that they had passed the cell

number of the person pretending to be Jaya to the local police who had said that they couldn't trace it since it was from a prepaid SIM. So, I just had to suck it up. Mr. Pereira hadn't actually said that, but that was the harsh reality.

I slid my phone out from under my pillow and started replying to messages from Reshma and Ayesha. They were both out at an ice cream parlor – our favorite one. I missed the little things so much. My life a year ago had been so spectacularly uncomplicated.

"Wish you were here," they had written on the photo they shared. It showed Priyanka, having just turned up, standing behind them. I replied with heart emojis. I wished I was there too. Anywhere but here.

I was totally caught up between feeling angry and feeling sorry for myself, and I couldn't decide on a course of action for either emotion. I hated the feeling that I was surrounded by people who were out to get me. Was Monica behind the cruel prank? Or was it someone else? I didn't like the idea that people in my class or school wanted to see me fail.

It made me feel like I was swimming with sharks.

"Hi, Dad," I said, putting him on speakerphone. He didn't usually call me mid-week.

"Bela, what is happening?" he enquired, annoyance in

his voice.

"With what, Dad?"

"Your grades. I had the results emailed to me. I was shocked."

"It's just a few tests," I snapped. "It's not a big deal."

"Yes, but the little ones lead to the big ones. Like streams lead to rivers and rivers to the sea."

Sophie grinned and I rolled my eyes. Of course I was mad at myself for doing so badly, but this had been such a difficult time. I would do better next time – I knew I would. Dad was just being...well, a dad.

"I'll make it up."

"Are you sure all that stuff with the Netflix show is not getting you down? Is Monica still bothering you?"

"The what? Oh no... I've forgotten all about that. Me and Monica are talking now. It's calm," I lied.

"Okay, if there is any problem or you need more books or extra tuition or anything else, let me know. You have a good opportunity here, Bela. The school is good and your future is good. I don't care much for movies, fame, stardom..." I could picture Dad counting these off on his fingers. "Education comes first. If you don't improve, I will take you out of the Academy. Back here, back to Reuben's high school."

Wow. Would he actually make me leave the Academy?

Wouldn't that be the ultimate fail?

If Dad decided I had to go home, I would have to go home.

Dad's words followed me as I slipped on my sneakers and cardigan and made my way downstairs. I knew my grades weren't good enough. I knew I had to try harder, do better. Back at my old school, I'd found schoolwork and exams a doddle. In fact, I used to revise for my tests and do my homework while hanging around at Mom's weekend dance classes. Now, I just couldn't concentrate on anything.

I stepped outside onto the carefully manicured grounds of the school and took a deep gulp of air into my lungs. Was I suffering from anxiety? I didn't actually know what that felt like and thankfully had never needed to find out. But there was something not right about how I was feeling, like I just couldn't cope with simple tasks in a simple day. I used to cleanse, tone and moisturize my skin each day. Nowadays, I didn't even care if I washed my face with soap. I was down to basics.

"Hey." There was a tap on my shoulder. I turned around, startled. It was Marc. I'd been making a conscious effort to stay away from everyone who had been on the outdoor shoot in Rajasthan the month before. I didn't think I could talk about it without breaking down.

"Hey, Bela. Alright?"

"Yeah, I'm good, thanks." I raised my eyebrows and smiled, trying to make myself look upbeat.

"I haven't seen you in the communal areas for a while... Where you off to?"

"Just some exercise," I said. "I haven't had a chance to move much lately. Been busy with studies."

He grimaced. "I know what you mean. Exams have been rough, girl. I didn't do so well in Biology – I only got 65%," he told me.

I died quietly inside. 65%? There was no way I was going to tell him that I was now a 26% girl.

"I didn't get what I'd hoped for either. I guess I needed to revise a bit more..."

We walked quietly for a few moments.

"Sophie seems to be managing fine though," I added, trying to break the silence. "She got good grades."

"Yes, but she isn't the star of a big Bollywood blockbuster, is she?"

"I'm not the star either," I reminded Marc. "It's you, remember!"

"You know what I mean," he said. "Your part is really important."

I nodded, although I wasn't convinced. I wondered

how much of it would end up on the cutting room floor.

"Hey, tell you what... Why don't we revise for next week's Geography and History exams together? Sometimes it helps to study with someone."

I was touched that Marc cared enough to want to revise with me. Maybe that would help pull me out of my slump? One thing was for sure: I had to improve – fast – if I wanted to stay at the Academy.

"Yes, why not?" I conceded. "The library?"

He nodded.

"Great," I replied.

There was an awkward silence.

"Bela, I'm sorry about what happened, you know? The whole hoax thing. It was really ugly."

I wasn't prepared for this conversation but I had nowhere to hide.

"I can't imagine what it would feel like – going all that way, missing the photo shoot, dealing with social media comments, and knowing everyone knows."

I simply nodded.

"But you can't hide away. It just gives more strength to whoever was behind it." He seemed to be scouring my face for a reaction. I wore my best poker face. "Do you know who it was?" he asked eventually.

"No idea," I replied, avoiding his gaze. "Could have

been anyone."

I had my suspicions, of course. As did Sophie and Tara. But we had no proof. How did Ajay know about the Om Shankara meeting when we hadn't announced it? Monica and her pals had been looking at me in the restaurant that morning as Ajay was talking to me about it. Then there was Monica running from the trailer back to the set at the very same time I had gotten the initial fake text from Jaya. Of course it didn't prove anything. But everyone else had been on set at the time...

I'm certain Mr. Pereira and Miss Takkar had the same idea. But would they take the risk of upsetting one of the major shareholders of the Academy over an inkling?

"It's done now," Mr. Pereira had told me when he'd called me into his office to talk it over. "I was inconvenienced too, Bela," he'd said. "But we've all learned a valuable lesson. Now, let's draw a line under this and move on."

*

At 4:45pm the following day, I made my way towards the Academy library, as promised. From my dorm, I had to go all the way down the winding staircase, past the TV Room and through the corridor where posters of 1990s Bollywood movies were displayed on the walls. I'd seen a few students boasting and pointing at their family members. My dream of one day being featured on these walls seemed to be just that – a dream. The reality was that I was struggling to even get a foothold in the Academy, let alone Bollywood.

I couldn't see anybody outside the library so, with some hesitation, I went in.

There were quite a few groups of students inside and right at the far end of the ground floor, in the corner by the window overlooking the cricket grounds, was Marc.

"Hi," I smiled. I put my bag down on the floor, being careful not to make a thud. The librarian was unforgivingly strict. She made Miss T seem like a pushover. We called her Moody Margaret although her name wasn't even Margaret. I had no idea how that came about.

My elementary school librarian had been so different. She used to love holding events and themed get-togethers in the library. We had so many dress-up days and fun moments in there. There was nothing close to that here.

"Hi," whispered Marc. He seemed to be in high spirits. "I've just finished my homework. Ready to revise?"

"Yep." I finally felt comfortable with Marc, like he was

an actual friend. I'd been so nervous around him just a few weeks earlier. It was great to feel that he was someone I could trust, especially when I was missing home and my old friends so much.

"What topic shall we hit first?" he asked.

"Well, in Geography we have a choice between Extreme Weather or Types of Soil."

Marc's head slumped down on the desk and he started laughing.

"Oh, man," he began. "A month ago, we were royalty living in a centuries-old Rajasthani palace. I had 200 foot soldiers guarding me. Now, my life is about differentiating between clay, sandy, loamy and silt."

It was so funny, we giggled, although I was careful not to laugh too loud.

"Share the joke, guys," came a voice I definitely wasn't longing to hear. Monica had walked in with A and B.

I pulled my revision cards out of my bag and started sorting them. They were actually organized perfectly but it was something to do.

"It's nothing. We're just revising for the exams next week," said Marc.

"Oh yeah, like you and I used to. Well, since you guys have taken up most of this table, I guess the girls and I will have to go upstairs."

"There are four spare seats here, Monica. You guys only need three," said Marc, leaning back in his chair.

Monica glanced at me with a look that said: *No chance I'm sitting anywhere near her...*

"Oh, I nearly forgot," she said, turning back on her heel as her friends made their way upstairs. "I got a sneaky preview copy for you. It hasn't even hit the shops yet."

"No way!" Marc exclaimed, looking pleased. "This is sick!"

The latest copy of *FilmGlitz* landed on the table, slap bang in front of me.

NEXT GEN SUPERSTARS

ran the headline. The cover image showed Marc and Monica on their thrones, with Ajay, Shamim and Deepa standing behind.

Marc picked it up and started flicking through, smiling and laughing with Monica at the feature stories inside. There were pages and pages of stunning images and interviews of the Academy kids who starred in *Jigsaw*.

All of them.

Except me.

TAKE FIFTEEN

I'd slept in again. It was becoming a bit of a habit but I felt so tired. The exams had taken a lot out of me but I was emotionally exhausted too.

I'd heard that the editing of *Jigsaw* was complete, and most of the participants were excitedly awaiting the trailer. I, meanwhile, was worrying over whether any of my scenes would make the final cut.

"Sorry, sir," I huffed as I walked in late to our Introduction to Cinematography class. Mr. Gupta, one of the oldest staff members, looked sternly at me before telling me to sit down.

I took the seat that Tara had saved for me, feeling sleepy, distracted and *so* not interested in learning about camera angles.

Tara passed me a note: *I got a warning for that YouTube clip. Coulda been worse.*

I turned it over and wrote back: *Oh no! Did your parents go mad?*

Nah, she scribbled. *I explained it to them. I think you-know-who complained or I would have gotten away with it.*

Tara subtly pointed at Monica who was sitting two

rows in front of us.

I furrowed my brow. That was unnecessary, especially considering Monica had done a hundred times worse to me. But was I even surprised that Monica wasn't the type of girl to let anything go unpunished?

"And what are we talking about when we say depth of field, Bela?" asked Mr. Gupta unexpectedly. I guess it was obvious I was miles away.

"Sorry, sir, can you repeat the question?" I asked, hurriedly squishing Tara's note and putting it into the pocket of my pants.

"What is depth of field?"

I shook my head. "Sorry," I said in a small voice. There was no point pretending I knew – Mr. Gupta would catch me out.

Tara raised her hand in a bid to rescue me.

"I know *you* know, Tara – you're planning to enroll in the Technical Department. I want to know if the Drama students understand."

A long, slender arm went up.

"Yes, Monica?"

Tara tapped me with her foot.

"It's a really basic thing that everyone should know," Monica began. The class laughed. I slid down a little into my chair.

"It refers to how blurry or sharp the image is around your main subject."

"Excellent!" enthused Mr. Gupta. "Of course you'd know, Monica," he chuckled. "You've grown up on film sets. Yes. Depth of field is the range of distance within which all objects will be in acceptable sharp focus."

I wasn't up to this. I didn't particularly like the technical subjects and I couldn't concentrate. I wasn't taking in much at all and had given up on writing notes.

But my senses came sharply into focus at the end of class.

"How many people know that the most successful film director in India, Om Shankara, actually started out as a cameraman?" asked Mr. Gupta.

A few students raised their hands, including – unsurprisingly – Monica. My heart threatened to leap out of my chest. I hoped nobody would mention *you-know-what*. I slid further down in my chair.

Mr. Gupta then filled us in on Om Shankara's ten-year career as a cinematographer before he went on to become a director. Monica's hand was still raised.

"Yes, Monica, what is it?" he asked.

"Sorry, sir," she said. "I know this has nothing to do with the class but I can't hold it in now that we're talking about him... Sir, I've just signed a role in Om Shankara's next movie!"

*

We hurried towards the cafeteria. My mind was still processing Monica's Breaking News. It felt like a punch to the stomach.

"No way!" said Tara, once we were sitting at the table in the farthest corner we could find. She waved at Sophie to come over. "You'll never guess what just happened, Soph!" she exclaimed, before proceeding to tell her the gossip with no commas or periods.

"She actually has a role in his movie?" Sophie looked gobsmacked.

"Yes! And I'm sure it was her who complained to the Academy about my impersonations. She can't even take a joke," Tara tutted, shaking her head.

"She even had the nerve to shove a presale copy of the *FilmGlitz* cover in Bela's face," Sophie added.

"When? You didn't tell me that, Bela!" scolded Tara.

"Oh, last week—"

"Talk of the devil," said Tara as she glimpsed Monica walking past our table. Tara didn't have much volume control.

"Sorry, did you say something?" asked Monica,

stopping dead in her tracks. A and B, who were behind her, bumped into each other as they came to an abrupt halt.

"Yeah, maybe I did," said Tara, standing up.

I noticed the usual background noise simmer down as people close by stopped talking.

"Tara, sit down," I implored. But she wasn't about to listen to me now.

"I heard you have a problem with me," Tara started.

"Why would I have a problem with you?" questioned Monica, eyes narrowing. "Remind me who you are?"

"Oh – *roasted!*" shouted Bahnaz as those within earshot laughed.

I gasped. Tara was just trying to stand up for me and now she was getting dragged into this sad, sorry state of affairs too.

I decided that things had gone far enough.

I was fed up with letting Monica get away with murder. I'd been at the receiving end of too much. Humiliating me in public, stealing lead songs and, I suspected, pulling cruel pranks. And now she was being rude to my friend.

She had to be told.

"Get a grip, Monica," I began. "Just because your parents were movie stars once-upon-a-time doesn't mean you can look down on everyone else. I've heard your 'I was born here – she's an outsider' comments and, you know what? They're pathetic!"

I was really angry now.

"As pathetic as your childish pranks," I continued. "At least I get chosen for film roles on merit. Would you have gotten even a single modeling assignment or movie role if it wasn't for your family? I'm not surprised that the whole world wants to kill nepotism in Bollywood when you're living proof of it!"

Monica's face dropped. She was thunderstruck. She clearly never thought I'd have the nerve to stand up to her. I hadn't thought I'd be able to either.

"That's uncalled for!" said Bahnaz, removing the sunglasses that were perched on top of her head. She shook out her mane of hair.

"Truth hurts, does it?" added Tara, keen to stay involved.

Monica ignored Tara completely. She was focused on me alone.

"You win a dance show, get bit parts in a couple of movies and think you're better than everyone else, don't you?" snarled Monica. "You think you can go around dissing me, mocking me, laughing at me..."

She took a deep breath in, trying to calm herself.

"You think you have a bigger role than me in *Jigsaw*? Well, Bela 'I-made-it-on-merit' Khanna," she said nastily, bending slightly so her face squared right up to mine. "Guess who's going to open the catwalk show at the movie premiere next month? It's me and Marc."

*

Getting to go home for two whole weeks once semester two had ended was my saving grace.

I felt bad for friends like Sophie and Tara – overseas students who had to spend the holidays at the Academy because home was too far away. I guess this was how they had both become so close.

So much had happened this year that I really needed the time to de-stress and just be me. I was totally enjoying seeing my besties again too. We were hanging out like the good old days even though I was a little lost at some of the things they dropped into conversation.

Being with my friends helped me stop thinking about the Academy, Monica and *Jigsaw*. Only one thing kept drawing me back into those thoughts, and that was the world premiere.

The film screening was just eleven days away and would open with the Mayuri Jain catwalk show and song and dance performances by the cast.

The marketing team was working overtime to make sure everyone knew about the show – it promised to be something totally different. *Jigsaw* was an unconventional Bollywood movie as it didn't have an A-list star cast. The producers needed to get as much pre-release publicity for the movie as they could.

So far, the hype had been impressive. First, there was that cover story in *FilmGlitz*, then hoardings across all the major cities in the country. The main movie poster featured Marc looking into a mirror, with Ganesh – the actor who played Vikram as a grown-up – looking back at him. I was happy for Marc. Nobody deserved the attention more than him.

The one thing that stung was that the catchy song *One, Two, Three, Naach!* that had been stolen from me and given to Monica *had* caught on. It was a huge hit, with the video registering half a million YouTube views over the four days since it had been released.

My family and I had watched it the very night it was aired. I was in the video but was completely overshadowed by Monica. I was just hoping that my solo dance in Rajasthan would catch on too.

"They're only inviting two of us?" asked Mom, looking at the *Jigsaw* world premiere invitation she had received in the mail. "What about the rest of the family?"

I frowned. It wasn't ideal but I guess they had to limit free tickets.

"You've never done a modeling show like this before, have you?" Mom went on. I eyed up the meal she was dishing up. Chicken balti and rice. It smelled so good.

"Nope," I replied. I could hear Daadi and Zara chuckling away in the living room as they watched a comedy. Since I'd been away, they had been spending a lot of time together. "I'm looking forward to the show, I guess."

"You guess?" Mom laughed. "Talk about laidback! I would have been beside myself at your age!"

Poor Mom. She really didn't know the half of it. I was going to play second fiddle to Monica for the third time now, although I was supposed to have had a bigger, better role than her. How was that even allowed?

Monica always got the star treatment, the most hype, the best opportunities. There were way better actors than Monica, and way better models. But you'd be forgiven for thinking that the casting directors had slim pickings.

Since I'd been back home, I'd glimpsed Monica on TV in an ad for sneakers. And when I'd gone into town with Daadi, Reuben and Zara, I'd seen an ad across the back of a bus where she was promoting a brand of candy.

Now, I could really understand why Jaymini quit the Academy and why Sophie had abandoned her dreams of being in front of the camera. The favoritism was really starting to wear me down.

My mood worsened as I tried to picture exactly what the catwalk show would be like. I started pushing the food around my plate rather than eating it.

"What's wrong, beti?" asked Mom gently.

"Nothing," I lied, like I had so many times before. "I just hope I don't fall over or anything."

"Of course you won't, Bela. You'll be great!"

Playing second fiddle to Monica was bad enough but what if she was planning another prank? The thought had been keeping me awake for the past few nights. The Om Shankara thing had been excruciating, and since I shamed her so badly in the cafeteria, she had real reason to get vicious now.

And if she did have another plan, this time there would be loads more people present. Celebrities, the press, even some politicians were scheduled to attend. I'd hate to be at the center of another public humiliation – especially when it was going to be broadcast live!

"Aah, why do you look so sad, Bels? Come here," said Mom, opening her arms wide to give me a big, warm hug.

"I'm fine, Mom. Really," I fibbed, putting my

enhanced acting skills to good use.

Mom kissed me on the forehead. "I know you're struggling," she said with tears in her eyes. "The world is like that, you know. It's not *what* you know, it's *who* you know. Opportunities are not equal, but I feel bad you had to realize this at such a young age. Perhaps I shouldn't have pushed you. I never wanted to be one of those pushy moms but maybe that's what I am, huh?"

"No, Mom!" I said, raising my voice a little. "That's not true."

"I just wanted you to be happy," she explained. "I wanted you to have the opportunities that I didn't get. You're a much better performer than I ever was, Bela. I hate the idea of your talent going to waste." Mom looked down.

I put my arms around her and squeezed her tight. "It isn't easy being there. I've had to adjust. But, you're right – if I hadn't gone on Dance Starz, hadn't gone to the Academy, I would never have been starring in movies, filming in Rajasthan or appearing in catwalk shows!"

Mom nodded. She wiped away a tear with the corner of her saree.

I ran to her bedroom and grabbed one of her old photo albums. I showed her the pictures of her dancing on stage in her school plays. Her face was so lit up. She looked so alive.

"I know you wanted this for yourself," I said. "It didn't work out for you but I'm so, *so* glad you pushed me to follow my dreams. So many girls like me aren't allowed to work in movies. I'm lucky to have parents who want the best for me."

"Yes, but is it what *you* want?" Mom asked, scouring my face for the truth.

"Of course!" I said instantly. "I love dancing and acting. It makes me feel like...me!"

I hoped I'd convinced Mom I was fine, even though I felt anything but.

As I lay in bed that night, I tried to look on the bright side. Even if I did eventually decide that the film industry and stardom weren't for me, at least I would have had a go at trying.

How many girls who fall in love with Bollywood could honestly say that?

*

My phone started ringing early in the morning. Or at least I thought it was early.

"Bela, I'm outside!"

It was Priyanka. It was 11am and I'd overslept again.

I rushed to the door and let her in.

"Wait in my room and I'll be there in a minute," I told her. I freshened up as quickly as I could.

"Now I can give you a hug," I said, grabbing her tightly.

"I was beginning to think we'd lost you," she smiled.

"Huh?" I looked away. I was pretty sure I knew what she meant.

"You were barely in touch with us at the end of the semester," she said, sitting on the edge of the bed. "We wondered if we were too 'ordinary' for you now." She smiled a sad smile.

It made me feel awful. All the time I had been worrying that my friends wouldn't understand what I was going through, I had failed to consider how they must be feeling.

"I'm so sorry, Pri," I said. "I missed you guys more than you know." Tears welled up. "It's just that… Where do I begin?"

"What's wrong, Bela?" she probed gently. "We've never gone so long without chats on the phone or over text before. I sensed you were avoiding us… You know you can tell me anything, right?"

I sighed. "What *isn't* wrong?" I answered eventually, not knowing where to start. "Academy life is *soooo* stressful... Movies are *soooo* stressful..."

I let it all out. I told her exactly what had been happening.

Priyanka lay down on my bed and laughed so hard when I got to the part about Monica in the cafeteria. Then she sat up and commented: "You actually said all that to her? In the lunchroom? No *way!* I wish I'd been there."

"You really don't," I told her. "I can't believe some of the things I said! It's just not me. Now all the people in the Academy will think I'm totally awful," I added, flopping back down on the bed and snuggling my face into my fluffy unicorn. "What have I become?" I moaned. "I wish I was still at your school. We had no worries back then."

Priyanka thought for a while and then spoke.

"So you're upset because you told Monica what you really think of her?"

I nodded.

"After she stole a lead song, made you run around Rajasthan while she took your part in the cover shoot, and will now be fronting the catwalk show when it should have been you?"

When she put it like that, I began to feel a little justified.

"You, girlfriend, need your head examined!"
concluded Priyanka. "You hated school. *We* hated
school. I still do! Now you have this amazing life with so
much excitement and opportunities. It's awesome you
told Monica what you think of her in front of all those
people! At least she won't pull another stunt again, will
she?"

"I wouldn't put it past her," I said, sitting up as
though I needed to prepare myself.

"But everyone will know it's her if she does anything
else," reasoned Priyanka. "Up until now, a few people
might have suspected she was behind everything, but it
would be too obvious now."

"I still don't have proof that she *was* behind
everything," I sighed. "Enjoying my misfortune is one
thing. Plotting it is another."

I stopped to think for a moment.

"Monica aside, the social media stuff is too much
sometimes," I confessed. "After all the fuss I made
about getting a phone, it's got to the point where I dread
switching it on sometimes. I mean, this one Bollywood
news feed was saying that my career would be over before
it even started as 'reality TV stars plummet as fast as
they rise.'" I paused. "It's hard to read that stuff..."

"Well then – don't," advised Priyanka. "You have

a choice. Instead, feel glad that they consider you important enough to write about in the first place. Plus, everything is so fast. My grandad always says that this morning's gossip is old news by the time evening comes around. It's not that big of a deal."

I could see her point.

"I would die to be in your shoes, you crazy girl," Priyanka continued. "I would die to be in the news and on all those Bollywood websites. But who wants to read about me? I would swap places with you right now – just like that!" She snapped her fingers.

I didn't say a thing. Somehow, my clever and pragmatic schoolfriend had just turned my mountain into a molehill.

Priyanka and I stayed in my room all day, chatting about anything and everything.

We talked about the time my mom came bursting into the classroom with a pair of shoes because they'd sent me to school in flip-flops, and the time Priyanka got detention for charging money to paint classmates' nails during break times. I was so glad to be able to laugh freely and not worry about who was watching, what Monica was up to, or what the rest of the world thought of me.

The time spent reminiscing with Priyanka flew by

and, before I knew it, her mom was at the door waiting to pick her up.

"We can't wait to see your next movie, Bela!" enthused Priyanka's mom, pinching my cheek really hard as though I was still nine years old. "Get my girl into the movies and you can both work together!"

"I would love that!" I said, giving Priyanka a warm hug and thanking her for the much-needed pep talk.

A weight had been lifted.

Priyanka was right.

Now that I'd had a taste of Academy life, I couldn't go back to my old one.

With opportunities come hardships. I was growing and learning.

And I was ready to make my mark at the *Jigsaw* world premiere.

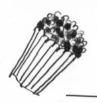

TAKE SIXTEEN

The day of the premiere was, as expected, chaotic. It was a Friday and, like the other Academy students involved in *Jigsaw*, I'd been granted a day off from classes (although I'd been told I'd have to catch up on the ones I missed).

The premiere was to take place on a specially erected stage outside Mumbai's famous Liberty Cinema. The art deco building was a century old but still looked so pretty with lots of fancy cosmopolitan restaurants, ice cream parlors and lush boutiques nestled around it. It was a popular area with young people so this was the perfect spot to attract the next generation of movie-goers.

I had to meet Sheetal at noon in one of the private rooms inside the cinema hall so we could do a run-through of the catwalk routine.

"The fashion show segment is quite short at just fifteen minutes but it will be the pièce de résistance," Sheetal told me. "I really wanted all of you to rehearse together but it's been impossible for various reasons – not least how small this room is," she said, looking around the cramped space. "So, we have to do all of you one by one."

I nodded. I was willing to do whatever it took to make this premiere successful. I was feeling a little more energized following my pep talks with Mom and Priyanka. Plus, I enjoyed seeing how excited Daadi, Reuben and Zara were, and how much everyone in Chandivali's Sector R2 was looking forward to the movie's release.

Cinema Factory had confirmed that they would only give us two complimentary tickets, and Mom and Dad couldn't afford the sky-high cost of entry for everyone. I was sad my family wouldn't be able to attend, but instead, they'd decided to create their own premiere at home, complete with popcorn and Mom's samosas. I knew my #friendslikefamily at home and at the Academy would be watching. They had been chattering about it all week.

Secretly, I was a little glad that they would be watching from afar. If something went wrong, it would look way worse in real life...

The rehearsal took no more than ten minutes. Sheetal was happy. "Good stuff, Bela," she said. "I know you haven't done a catwalk before but I really don't think it's a problem for you, being such a great dancer."

She wished me luck and pointed me to a long corridor

which led to the dressing rooms and backstage area, called the Amber Lounge.

I heard footsteps behind me and before I could turn, somebody had covered my eyes with big hands.

"Guess who?"

I knew that voice! "Monty!" I said. He proceeded to give me a bear hug. I was so happy to see him. True to form, Monty looked fabulous in his paisley patterned suit plus rainbow badge, of course. I couldn't imagine many people carrying that off so stylishly.

"Lovely to see you again, Monty," said Miss T, brushing past. "Will someone from your team do Bela's makeup now?"

"Someone from my team?" he retorted. "No, *dahling!* I'm doing Bela's hair and makeup myself."

I was delighted. It gave me an opportunity to fill him in on all the drama I'd been engulfed in. He listened carefully while expertly doing me up.

"You know what, Bela?" Monty said simply, adding finishing spray to my curls. "There's a saying: what doesn't kill you makes you stronger. I learned it was true very early on. You're still here, so you're stronger now than you were when I first met you. Believe me, I can see it."

As Monty applied some blusher to my cheeks, I

checked my reflection. I did look a little older, a little wiser than I had when I had started out on this movie.

I'd grown with *Jigsaw*.

It was time to celebrate.

*

By 6pm, the street outside Liberty Cinema was thronging with TV crews, photographers, journalists, bloggers, vloggers and members of the public.

I stood on the red carpet outside the movie theater alongside the other Academy students. I felt so excited. For *Mystery*, there had been a low-key screening and I hadn't been invited. This felt really glamorous, like the kind of movie premiere you see on TV.

Deepa, Monica and I had drop-dead gorgeous dresses to wear – gold satin gowns with pleats at the waist, pockets, and a full skirt with train – from Mayuri Jain, of course. Marc, Shamim and Ajay wore slick black suits, gold shirts and black ties and looked so much older than eighth graders.

Most of the photographers were after shots of Monica. She was the most well-known cast member from the Academy, after all. Marc, as the lead, was being interviewed by a foreign television channel.

Some of the seniors in the movie were highly respected actors. I wished my parents and Daadi could have been there to see them. Ganesh, the movie's adult Vikram, had a swarm of people around him, eager for quotes and autographs.

Yogi rushed by with some guests and asked the ushers to lead them to their seats. He caught sight of me and told me to give them my autograph. My hand shook as I signed their *Jigsaw* premiere program guides. *Why does he want me to do that?* I wondered. I wished I'd come up with a fancier signature.

"Ten more minutes here," Miss T informed us. She was wearing a halterneck navy blue tea dress. Her hair had been done up in a classic Hollywood style with cascading curls – she looked like a star. She seemed to be enjoying the attention too. "Then we'll be going inside to get you all changed for the show. But first, *FilmGlitz* wants a photo with the Academy girls together."

Oh no, I thought to myself. Not *FilmGlitz*!

Deepa and I were positioned on either side of Monica. I straightened my back, conscious of being dwarfed by her in every sense of the word. I forced as wide a smile as I possibly could and tried not to blink when the cameras flashed – there was nothing worse than a photo with eyes shut.

"Smile, Moni!" came a voice. I turned and saw Malaika Rani, Monica's mom. "Do us proud! Maybe move forward a little?"

Monica made a loud tutting noise.

The photographer stopped, as though he wasn't sure whether to obey Monica's wishes or her mom's. He indicated with his hands for Monica to come forward but she stayed put. Malaika Rani stayed on the sidelines watching her daughter keenly but, to Monica's relief, she was soon shown the way to her front row seat.

I didn't even care if I was in the center, front or side. I had stopped wanting to be more important or more special than any other Academy girl. I just wanted the event to go without a hitch, without any awkward scenes or embarrassment.

"Okay, that's the lot," said a man dressed in a black suit, holding a walkie-talkie. We were steered toward the large double doors that led to the Amber Lounge by a group of backstage dressers.

"Stop herding us around like cattle," snapped Monica. "How about telling us where to go and we'll make our own way there?"

"Speak with respect, Monica," reprimanded Miss T. "You're an Academy student here – not Shashi Kumar's daughter!"

One of the dressers obviously agreed. She stopped to look at Monica in a who-do-you-think-you-are? kind of way, but decided against actually saying it. Instead, she responded in a passive-aggressive tone: "Madam, kindly head toward the Amber Lounge. Once you get there, wait for further instructions."

Monica obviously didn't like that and wasn't about to wait for anyone. She broke away toward the lounge in a huff.

We followed behind at the same time that Mayuri Jain – dressed impeccably in a feathery cream and turquoise gown – took to the stage. I was grateful for all the speakers and mini screens backstage, ensuring we didn't miss a second of the action. I was really starting to look forward to seeing the final movie along with the five hundred or so fans who had bought tickets for the event. I could feel the energy of the crowds as they started to arrive. Everyone's adrenaline levels were nudging higher as we got closer to the show's kickoff.

"I'd like to welcome you to the show and say a big thank you to the *Jigsaw* cast members who are giving up their time to model my creations on this stage," began Mayuri, her crystal chandelier earrings glistening as she turned her head from left to right.

The audience cheered loudly to show their

appreciation.

"But before we start the catwalk show and lead on to the highly anticipated screening of *Jigsaw*, I'd like to tell you a little about my journey in this industry. So I can inspire others. I started with nothing..."

Her speech was long. And Mom was right – Mayuri really was trying to convince the world that she had not benefited from nepotism.

"So, whether you're an insider or an outsider," she concluded as I reached the Amber Lounge, "as long as you love Bollywood and have talent and fire in your heart, there is a place for you here."

The spectators clapped and whistled, perhaps in a show of sympathy for the criticism she had received recently. Whatever she really was – outsider or insider – Mayuri was a success and I was glad she had said that what mattered most was talent.

As Mayuri wrapped up her life story and made her way from the stage to the long row of seats running alongside the catwalk, my nerves began to jangle. We were due on in twenty minutes.

We had been arranged into groups and asked not to move. There was a lot going on around us, with people shouting orders at each other and talking through their headsets to the technical team outside. The noise from the audience seemed to be increasing, almost drowning out the sound of the clothing rails being wheeled from one side of the dressing room to the other, each garment labeled carefully.

"This one is for you, Bela," I was told by one of the assistants as she handed me my catwalk costume. We were only modeling one outfit each so I was really glad I loved it. The fusion gown was baby pink in color with an A-line cut. The ethnic embellishment around the neckline made it look like it was fit for any occasion – casual or dressy.

I took the dress and draped it over my arm. It was much heavier than I had imagined, caused by all the fabulous layers of tulle under the skirt, I suspected.

I discreetly looked over at the dress Monica had been given. It was the same color as mine but it appeared to be a strapless, satin mermaid gown with so much fabric – a huge train perhaps? I adored my dress but I was really crushing over Monica's.

Back in the Amber Lounge, I grinned when I glimpsed the host – Raman Sood – take the mic. He would forever be associated with one of the best nights of my life.

He enthusiastically greeted the audience and then welcomed onto the stage our Principal, Mrs. Arora, who thanked the producers for giving her students this once-in-a-lifetime chance. The Academy students all cheered loudly for her, which I thought was a heart-warming gesture. She looked a little overwhelmed, standing there in front of what was now a sea of faces.

It was a short speech but it made me surprisingly emotional. Despite all the highs and lows, we really were blessed to be students of such an incredible school. I looked around and it wasn't just me – Miss Takkar and Mr. Pereira also looked close to tears. Deepa, I was sure, was wiping her eyes with her hand. I realized I knew so little about her, even though we were sharing something so big.

After one of the playback singers from the *Jigsaw* soundtrack had sung two of the songs live on stage, there was a short commercial break. I could feel the excitement and tension building up backstage. The stage manager was engaged in final checks, absolutely focused and concentrated. The audience members chatted noisily to one another while the Pepsi ad played out.

When the ad came to an end, one final vocalist was invited on stage to a wave of applause. This was the moment I had to suck some air into my lungs to try to calm my nerves. He was the last act before the main attraction – us!

Although "the walk" I had rehearsed for the show

with Sheetal was child's play compared to the steps I had performed in dances, I was trembling. I was acutely aware that Monica was a pro at the catwalk. She was casually giggling away with Marc as though she was in the school lunch line.

For me, the occasion was huge! The more I thought about it, the more nauseated I felt. I fanned my face with my hands. I really didn't want any stage shine!

Miss T and two of the ushers made all six of us line up neatly, again telling us not to disappear to the restrooms or anywhere else until our stint was over.

Monica huffed. She really didn't like being told what to do. Marc put a friendly arm around her shoulder to calm her down and she seemed to relax. *What an unlikely friendship*, I thought to myself. I buffed my nails with my fingertips, trying to keep busy.

"Right, everyone!" shouted Sheetal as she gave us all a last-minute pep talk. "It's the first time such an event has happened here, so let's make it one to remember. Make sure you stay within the confines of the LED lights on the stage – we don't want anyone tumbling off! Most importantly, remember to enjoy yourselves!"

As Monica had kindly informed me in the cafeteria, she would be opening the show with Marc. This was confirmed by the call sheet which told me I would be going on straight after them. Deepa, Ajay and Shamim would follow behind me, then we would all go back on and dance together to *One, Two, Three, Naach!*, take a final bow, and then clear the stage for the senior actors to take the ramp.

Knowing I would go on alone, just before Deepa, Ajay and Shamim, made me feel a little special. It didn't help the butterflies much though.

Monica was positioned directly in front of me, her hand perfectly positioned on her hip. This was a stroll in the park for her.

I took some deep breaths. *Don't mess up, Bela*, I told myself. *You have one job to do – walk out there, walk back!*

"Relax, Bela," said Deepa, as if reading my mind. "It'll be fine and you'll be lucky to get your part over and done with before us!"

"Thanks," I smiled, fiddling nervously with my hair.

I could hear the singer hitting the final few notes of his last song. We were due on any second.

"And now, the moment you have all been waiting for," announced Raman Sood, his voice booming. "Opening the show for us tonight are the junior actors from *Jigsaw*. They are all students at the Bollywood Academy. Thank you to the prestigious school for all their assistance in allowing this movie to be made."

Through the gap in the curtain, I could see Miss Takkar, Mrs. Arora and Mr. Pereira standing up, receiving the applause with thanks.

I was pleasantly surprised to see how many people had turned up – the numbers had swelled in the time we had been backstage. Realizing that there wasn't an empty seat in sight, and that there were hordes of people gathered behind the barriers without tickets trying to get a look-in, made me happy and giddy all at the same time. Yogi was clapping zealously, full of confidence at seeing such a great turnout for the show.

The stage, with its glass floor edged with twinkling LED lights, looked so modern and chic. Marc and Monica stood ready in the center. The music started to blare out and the curtains began to separate.

Monica swung her hips expertly from side to side as she set off. Marc had that cool, teenage guy walk down to a T. They stopped once, half-way down the ramp, to turn, snap their fingers, turn again, and then continue.

I shuffled forward to prepare myself for my entrance.

Monica was gliding gracefully to the front of the stage, full of self-assuredness, flashing her pearly whites in every direction for the onlookers. Many of them had their phones in the air, eager to capture the memory. She turned to wave to a group of youngsters screaming her name, while Marc raised his hands above his head and cheered.

And then, as if in slow motion, the train of Monica's billowing satin dress got caught under her heel. My eyes widened and my mouth dropped open as I saw her long arms start flailing around as she tried to regain her balance.

There were gasps from the audience. Monica was just a few yards from the front of the stage and she was going down… Before anyone could take a step, she had landed flat on her backside.

Cameras were clicking furiously and I could see their blinding flashes. This was *the* event of the evening, and the photographers knew it. The TV cameras were avidly recording every second of the incident.

I only had one second to make a decision.

This was the moment my star would eclipse Monica's.

This was the moment she would be put in her place once and for all – payback for all the times she had mistreated me and put obstacles in the path of my dreams.

This was the moment I would finally rise in this unforgiving industry and she would fall.

There would never be an opportunity like this again.

But did I want to be that girl?

I dropped my shoulders and straightened my back, waltzing onto the stage earlier than my cue.

"What are you doing?" someone called from behind me. But it was too late to turn back. I had made up my mind.

I put on a comic expression and wobbled down the ramp. I wasn't expecting the music to be so loud or the catwalk so long. Plus, I had come out earlier than I was supposed to so I hadn't even rehearsed to the beats that now hammered in my ears.

Almost as loud as the music was the sound of the audience laughing at Monica. Marc had finally noticed Monica on the floor and he looked like he was in quicksand. He appeared rooted to the spot, totally lost.

Adrenaline kicked in. I had to be quick or my improvised plan wouldn't work.

I walked as fast as I could and just before I reached the front of the stage, I waved my arms around in an exaggerated motion and forced myself to fall.

I landed next to Monica, who was trying to get up. She looked so bewildered, her face pale and helpless with shock.

The crowd seemed to stop laughing, wondering whether this was all a deliberate act.

I smiled at Monica and managed to say "Stay there"

through my teeth.

She took the hint. Pulling herself together, she attempted to stand up and then pretended to slip, screaming "Ouch!" and rubbing her behind as she did so. People cheered.

I glimpsed Malaika Rani. She was standing up, one hand over her forehead and the other over her mouth, unsure whether to be horrified or amused. Shashi Kumar grabbed her arm, forcing her to sit down.

The audience then started clapping and whistling as they focused on something behind me. I turned back.

There was Deepa, comically sashaying down the ramp with a wonderful expression on her face. A few seconds later, she planted herself flat on her backside right next to me.

An hour or so before, the three of us had been posing for top showbiz photographers. Now, here we were, sitting in a heap on the floor on the spot-lit stage. The spectators were loving it, clapping along rhythmically, miraculously convinced that this was all a light-hearted act.

A few beats later, Ajay and Shamim strode onto the catwalk. Shamim extended a hand out to me while Ajay did the same to Deepa.

Marc reached out to Monica.

They pulled us up.

We all joined hands together and took a bow as the audience whooped with joy. Miss Takkar and Mr. Pereira were applauding hard.

The music was still going so we all started dancing to *One, Two, Three, Naach!*, encouraging the audience to join in. We snapped our fingers up to the right, down to the left, shook our hips, jumped and jived.

Shamim smiled at me. We were all on cloud nine, totally reveling in the moment. I was amazed to see that most of the audience knew the moves already and the ones who didn't were giving it their best shot!

We laughed, we pouted, we smiled, we posed, we celebrated. It was so much fun, and it finally felt like being part of a team. We were in it together, entertaining the crowd and doing what we loved.

When the host thanked us over the mic and we began to make our way backstage, I stopped and blinked. Was I dreaming? For there, in the fifth row, were Mom, Dad, Zara, Reuben, Daadi, Priyanka, Ayesha, Reshma, Uncle Manoj, Auntie Brinda and Rimpi. They were waving a banner that said "We Back Bela!"

I cupped my hands over my mouth. Emotions got the better of me as happy tears filled my eyes. Wiping them away with my fingertips, I realized that there was one other person I hadn't seen before. Somehow, I knew who she was. Jaya. She had come! Had she paid for everyone's tickets?

I waved manically at them, sending them flying kisses and then putting my hand to my heart. I loved them all so much. They were my strength. They had kept me going.

I hoped I had done them proud.

Once backstage, I was overcome with a mix of emotions. Had I done the right thing out there after Monica fell? Would Sheetal be mad at me? What about the teachers? Fear gripped me momentarily.

"You were a lifesaver, Bela!" exclaimed Marc, hugging me. "What the heck? My mind went totally blank out there."

"Really?" I asked, still not daring to feel relieved just yet. "I just did what I felt I had to."

Sheetal ran over to me. She got down on one knee and clasped her hands together. "Thank you for saving my show," she said, tears brimming in her eyes.

"Oh no, please don't," I said, amazed that my scheme seemed to have worked. "I wasn't sure..."

She stood up and hugged me tight. "You saved the day! The audience actually fell for it – pardon the pun!" Sheetal guffawed, obviously delirious. "No, seriously,

I would have been in big trouble! What you guys did without planning was just ace. Improvising like that, working as a team... Thank you all."

I peered over Sheetal's shoulder and saw Monica looking at me. I froze, not knowing what to expect. Was she thinking that I did it to be a hero? Was this going to backfire on me too, like everything else?

To my utter amazement, she mouthed the words "Thank you."

She walked over to me.

"Bela," she said in an uncharacteristically quiet voice. Everyone around us stopped chattering and strained hard to listen in.

Monica paused, tapping the side of her head with her long fingers as though searching for the right words. She let out a huge sigh. "I tell you, that would have been the end of my modeling career. Falling on a ramp is every model's worst fear. You saved my skin. You have no idea... You saved the show."

I exhaled, finally. "Don't mention it," I replied. "It was a gamble. I could easily have ended up making it worse."

She grinned and then quickly turned serious. She motioned with her head for me to move a few steps to one side.

"I feel pretty stupid about, you know, everything

that's happened," she said, sounding so different to the girl I knew. "I got carried away by what everyone told me. Of all people, I should have known not to believe everything I heard or read!" Monica was moving her hands around a lot. I didn't think I'd ever seen her nervous before. "I didn't like how you thought I only got jobs because of my parents..."

"I'm sorry–" I interjected. But Monica seemed keen to get things off her chest.

"I believed you thought you were a better actor than me. When I saw you'd been mocking me and laughing at me on YouTube, I got mad. It was childish," she continued, looking down. "Anyway, thanks again for what you did just now. Not sure I deserved it, to be honest, after Rajasthan."

Was Monica admitting to something?

"It's okay," I said, feeling stunned that she was opening up to me. "I was pretty rude to you in the cafeteria. Maybe we should call it quits and forget about what's happened in the past?"

Forgetting about all those separate incidents would be no easy task. The whole time I had been feeling so low, I had also been questioning myself. I had wondered if I was weak. If I had been to blame for what was happening to me. If I would always be an easy target.

TAKE SIXTEEN

Now I realized that the moment I had made the decision to save Monica when she fell, was the moment I had made the decision to stand up for myself.

"Sounds like a great idea to me," smiled Monica. "Oh, and one other thing," she added. "Om Shankara…"

My face went as pale as a ghost.

"Don't worry," she said, putting a hand on my arm. "It's nothing bad! I've been offered a huge modeling assignment by Versace. They want me to be the face of one of their teen brands and the shoot is in Italy! So I can't do Uncle Om's film."

"Oh," I said. I pursed my lips, confused about why she was sharing this information with me and not sure what to say next. "I'm sorry," was all that came out.

"No, it's fine. My choice," she beamed. "Although Mom's desperate for me to do the movie. I can put in a little word for you though? You'll have a good shot at it, especially since Yogi has been raving about your solo dance."

"You've seen it?" My jaw dropped. I couldn't believe my dance had made the final cut!

"Yeah, it's great," she smiled as my heart hit a speed of two hundred beats a minute.

Monica grabbed my arm and linked it with hers.

I grinned in disbelief at what was happening. We

257

both headed back outside to the red carpet and as we reappeared, the snappers leaped into action.

They wanted to capture the mood and the moment.

An outsider in step with the biggest insider in Bollywood would make a very rare shot indeed.

THAT'S A WRAP

Acknowledgements

This book would not have come to life without the incredible Lantana Publishing.

It's a real honor that *Starlet Rivals* was chosen to be the first fiction title of this most progressive and forward-thinking publisher.

Founder Alice Curry shared my excitement for *Starlet Rivals* from the day I submitted my manuscript. It's been quite a journey! Alice helped me to polish both the concept and the script with real encouragement. She also gave me a star editor – a big hug to Lucy Rogers for all the fine-tuning and to Natasha Arora as shadowing editor for suggesting where I needed to add extra "masala" to the text.

A special mention for Jen Khatun's awesome illustrations – I'm totally in love! Seeing them for the first time made me feel so emotional.

Thank you to my husband Jas and my children – Roma, Arjun, Mili and Tara – for their tireless support and enthusiasm for the Bollywood Academy. Their belief in this project allowed me to keep on dreaming.

A special thanks to my generous mother-in-law for the endless home-cooked meals that spared me time to write.

Above all, thank you to Bollywood, for the music, the magic, and the memories.

About the author

Puneet Bhandal grew up in West London as a huge fan of Bollywood cinema but struggled to find anything to read that would connect her to her country of origin.

Her first writing job was as a Bollywood film journalist for a London-based newspaper. As the Entertainments Editor of *Eastern Eye*, Puneet enjoyed behind-the-scenes action on Bollywood movie sets. The Bollywood Academy was born from her observations of real-life Bollywood personalities – both insiders and outsiders!

Puneet loves being in Bela's world and introducing young readers to the fascinating Indian film industry.

She particularly loves interweaving fact with fiction; while Jal Mahal is a real-life palace in Rajasthan, the 5-star hotel is imagined, and while Chandivali Sector R2 is a bustling Mumbai suburb, Kohinoor island, where the Academy is situated, is an imaginary location.

Puneet has spent more than 20 years working as a journalist and editor for a range of newspapers, books and magazines. She has also founded her own occasionwear boutique, with her dresses featured in *Vogue*, *Hello!* and other fashion magazines. "Miss England 2019" chose to wear one of her dresses at the competition finals! One of her favorite jobs is running Bollywood-themed creative writing workshops for schools – complete with a Bollywood dance lesson!

About the cover artist

Jen Khatun is a children's book illustrator of Bangladeshi/Indian heritage who grew up loving all the costumes, dance sequences, and songs from the countless Indian Bollywood movies she watched as a child. Jen lives and draws by the coast of East Sussex.